NEITHER SOPHISTICATED
NOR
INTELLIGENT

Great hanging
out w/ you
All. Next time
we should keep
our clothes on.

NEITHER SOPHISTICATED NOR INTELLIGENT

A College Humorist's Take on Life

Lee Camp

CONTENTS

INTRODUCTION
+ ACKNOWLEDGEMENTS
= INTROLEDGEMENTS

When I was in my first year of college, I had to write a ten page paper for a history class. I worked extremely hard on the paper and then confidently submitted it. It was returned to me with a big, fat "C-" on the front (it was indeed big and fat – measuring nearly three inches across). The highlight of the written comments from my professor was the part that read, "This paper is neither sophisticated nor intelligent." Apparently my professor failed to realize that nothing one does in college is sophisticated or intelligent. Anyway, I am proud to say that I have now taken all of my unsophisticated, unintelligent thoughts and put them into a book. As for the cover drawing, you'll have to read further to figure out the meaning behind that.

This book is composed of humor columns, fiction writing, cartoons and Top 7 Lists. That's right, I said, "Top 7 Lists." The way I see it, at least three out of every top 10 list are not very funny. So, I cut those three unfunny selections out of all my top 10 lists. This results in highly efficient, extremely humorous, easily portable Top 7 Lists.

The humor columns presented in the following pages were first published in the University of Virginia's newspaper, *The Cavalier Daily*. I thank the staff of the *Cav Daily* for their help and for giving a lowly humor columnist a chance. Most of the editing for this book was done by the lovely and talented Ryann Collins, and I thank her sincerely for all her work. Of course, I must take full credit for any and all grammatical errors, except two that are up to your choosing. I also want to thank Ryann for motivating and inspiring me to put this book together.

All the cartoons including the cover were drawn by the lovely and talented Dean Camp, and I thank him sincerely as well. He is an incredible artist and is available for wedding receptions and children's birthdays. I also want to thank my parents, my older brother, my grandparents and my dog for helping me learn comedy and supplying me with endless material.

I'm fairly certain the content of this book is funny and occasionally downright hilarious. So, if you're not laughing, it doesn't make you a bad person, but it does mean there's something tragically wrong with your sense of humor. Seek therapy, and once you've got that cleared up, enjoy!! (Don't you hate excessive exclamation points?!!)!

7 Rejected Titles for This Book

1. Oprah's Favorite Book Ever Ever
2. Lee Camp Slept Here (and we still haven't gotten the smell out of the sheets)
3. 'Sorry I Ran over Your Dog' and Other Hallmark Greeting Card Sayings
4. Don't Buy This Book! (It will be the worst decision you ever make.)
5. Harry Potter and The Mystical World of Opium
6. Crap Written in My Spare Time
7. DAVE BARRY Had Nothing to Do with This Book

1
College

Learning Is Overrated

Seeing as I spent a whopping four whole years in an institution of higher learning (although some see it as an institution of learning while you're high), I figured I would relay what I learned in my first year to other young adults who are just beginning college. I've put some quick pointers about the first year of college into an easy-to-follow, readily-accessible, handily-organized literary travel-pack. Enjoy it or give it to a friend for his Bar Mitzvah.

First: Pack a lot of underwear, and if you are matched with a random roommate, do an extensive criminal background check on him or her. Before I left for school I had to make several arrangements, say goodbye to all my friends and pack every pair of underwear I had ever owned. Then I started worrying about what my roommate was going to be like. With my luck, I figured my roommate's hobby would be cultivating highly toxic bacteria on *my* desk even though he would assure me they weren't dangerous unless I "upset them." Actually my roommate was pretty cool. I called him over the summer so that we could decide what we were going to bring. Like most freshmen we wanted to split up who had to bring each major appliance such as television, refrigerator and microwave popcorn. Here's how we split them up:

What My Roommate Brought	*What I Brought*
microwave	
television	
VCR	
minifridge	
speakers	
stereo	
Sega Genesis	
coffee maker	broom

(When reading this chart, keep in mind that it was a very nice broom with angled bristles for easy cleaning. This is not to say that during my college years I ever used the broom or any complicated cleaning device of its kind.)

Second: When moving into college, watch your parents at all times because they may try to do something tragic such as put stuff away neatly. Moving in basically consisted of trying to carry twice my weight in school supplies with most of the sharper devices digging into my arms and chest. Once my family and I had piled everything into my room, my parents put it all away neatly so that I could pull it all out into a big pile over the course of the following two days. We then tried several different furniture arrangements. We put the desk on the left and the bed on the right. Then we put the bed on the left and the desk on the right. Then we put the desk on the bed and the bed in the stairwell. We found this gave me the most room.

Third: Beware of the "Fun Fests" or something similar. Just about every college plans some sort of festivities for new students. The "Fun Fests" at my college were a lot like the "Spring Fling" at my elementary school. You could bounce around inside a Moon Walk, you could enjoy cotton candy and you could walk around for hours not sure you're having fun but assuming you must be because everybody else looks like they're experimenting with mind-altering drugs.

Then there was the pseudo-free stuff that was being handed out. This is stuff that appears to be free but actually entails being harassed by a company for the rest of your natural life and possibly decades thereafter. For example, at one table a guy was offering people bags of cookies if they would fill out an application for a credit card. He said, "You're not ordering anything. It's just an application." And he's telling the truth – it's an application for full time harassment by a credit card company. Is that really worth a little baggy of stale cookies? Now you know how desperate college kids are for food.

Fourth: No matter how your college works its class scheduling, you will most likely never get any of the courses you want. By the time I was allowed to select my classes during my first year, the only classes remaining were those that began at four in the morning and/or involved Scottish folk dancing.

However, during the first day of classes I learned that it doesn't matter what you've signed up for in advance because the tentative scheduling book you receive before school starts usually has as much to do with the *actual* schedule of classes as the menu at Wendy's. My first day of classes basically just consisted of showing up to a room full of students who had never even heard of the class that I was there to attend. After several days of heated arguments with the recorded voice on the automated scheduling system, I was able to get some of the classes I wanted to take. Here's my schedule for every Monday:

> 4:00—4:50 a.m. Scottish Folk Dancing
> 5:30—6:45 a.m. The History of Scottish Folk Dancing
> 8:00—8:50 a.m. Scottish Folk Dancing in The Modern World
> 11:00—11:50 a.m. Philosophy 137: The Effect of Scottish Folk Dancing on Humanity

Well, that's all I learned in my first year of college. Pretty pathetic, isn't it? Actually, learning this much my first year at school is pretty impressive when you consider the fact that I didn't learn anything in the following three years. In fact, I don't even remember two of them.

7 Things Learned at College

1. When ketchup can serve as an entree
2. The entire schedule of the Cartoon Network
3. Origami—how to make a shot glass out of a diploma
4. What to wear to achieve optimal speed when going down a Slip N' Slide covered in whipped cream
5. Peaceful coexistence with hung-over roommates
6. Excuses for coming home the next morning with the same clothes on
7. How to describe hitting on women as an extra-curricular activity on a resume

A 6'4 Grandma from The University of Virginia

A few years ago I took my grandmother to a University of Virginia football game because she wanted to watch a game and because fighting the drunk crowd by myself was no longer challenging. Instead of actually watching some football, I spent the entire game protecting my grandmother from extremely dangerous threats such as hotdog vendors.

My grandmother and my younger brother showed up for the game bright and early one Saturday morning with enough food to feed a group of adult Clydesdales. The first problem of the day was created by a juice box. Growing up in a society based on the marvels of the juice box, I assumed that every animal above the level of marsupial had been introduced to its intricate workings. However, my grandmother actually grew up before the time of the juice box. This established, it seems a little more plausible that the first thing she did when handed a juice box was begin to rip open the top with the strength of several hungry sabertoothed tigers. I showed her how to insert the straw, and as I handed it back to her I warned, "Don't squeeze it because it will squirt you." Presumably hearing my warning but choosing to live on the edge, my grandmother grabbed the juice box with all authority, firing orange Hi-C into her lap. I think we're all a little wiser from that experience.

After lunch, even though it was still two hours before the game, my grandmother wanted to head straight to the stadium. We arrived while fans from last week's game were still leaving. Unfortunately my grandmother had filled a grocery bag with leftover corned beef and jellybeans, and at the gate we were informed that outside food was not allowed inside the stadium. I assume this is to force fans to pay three dollars for a bottle of water. (Is there any other more ubiquitous, life-sustaining natural resource for which we can be charged? Water literally falls from the sky in great quantities, and we're paying for it.) My grandmother was not about to give up corned beef; so she got into a heated discussion with the senior citizen gentleman manning the gate. Soon enough she was strutting into the stadium, food in hand, with a "still got it" look on her face.

There are basically two places our tickets allowed us to sit – either the student section or "the hill." "The hill" is a large area of grass at one end of the field which got its name from the fact that it's, you guessed it, a hill. It was easy to get a good spot on the hill because nobody except janitorial staff had arrived at the game yet. As we waited, I realized that the hill actually has a fairly steep slope, hence the name "hill." This type of slope is not good for sitting because you slowly slide down the hill while your pants remain where they are, creating a wedgie factor equivalent to hanging from a flagpole by your belt loop. I thought that maybe this wasn't the best spot for my grandmother. Luckily, it appeared there were some bleachers at the far left end of the student section where we could avoid being mobbed by crazed fans, shirtless guys with letters painted on their chests and testosterone levels higher than an entire professional wrestling audience. We moved to the bleachers.

To my dismay, just as we sat down a herd of students filled the seats around us (they travel in packs). Of course, right as the game started everybody between us and the field stood up, leaving us with nothing to watch but Abercrombie khaki pants. My grandmother didn't complain, but I knew I couldn't make her stand through the entire game. She kept an optimistic view. In fact, she said to me, "I'm sure they will SIT DOWN soon! I can't imagine these people in front of us will BLOCK OUR VIEW for the entire game!" My little brother and I scanned the hill for an open spot, but the hill was now packed. It looked like a picture from *Where's Waldo?* and trying to find a spot was like trying to find Waldo's lost shoe. My brother went out and hiked through the entanglement of people, eventually finding a spot, which I helped my grandmother crowd surf over to. I felt like I was in the old show "American Gladiators." (I think it would have spiced up that show if the gladiators had to help their grandmothers through the obstacle courses.) We finally sat down, relaxed and began to watch the backside of the portly cameraman who was on a platform in front of us. He created a total eclipse of the game.

At halftime we moved to another spot that was out of the umbra of the cameraman's shadow. The new spot wasn't that bad until the fourth quarter when apparently recess began, and every kid below the age of twelve started running around wildly. Paper airplanes, empty water bottles and many types of food rained down all around us. Then in a cooperative effort, the members of The Association of Extremely High Pitched Little Girls began shrieking. We were sitting in the middle of a frenzied ant hill of kids scurrying around hitting each other. It's been scientifically proven that young boys and many adult men are twice as likely to run around like idiots after watching more than an hour of football. Apparently the male mind thinks, "Look! All those guys on the field are running around knocking over other guys. Why aren't I?" This thought is immediately followed by a striking blow to whomever is standing nearby. Needless to say all this made for a great atmosphere for a grandmother. We ended up leaving the game a little early in order to salvage our sanity.

Here's an updated list of great achievements by senior citizens in the past century.

1. John Glenn goes back into space.
2. Bob Dole runs for president.
3. My grandmother survives a college football game.

The Battle of Who Can Clean Less

There is an extremely pressing situation affecting our lives right now. Hundreds have died senselessly or been seriously injured, and children run in fear when confronted with the atrocities of which I am about to speak. That's right, I'm referring to the overall nastiness that has enveloped my apartment like a cup of thick New England clam chowder slowly drowning a struggling fly. My roommates and I, like the fly, have worked endlessly to fight off the deluge of grime and clam chowder that has soaked our wings and entangled our spiny legs until we've choked on chunky bits of clam. (I lost sight of this analogy long ago, so let's move on and never again speak of what just transpired.)

However, I must say that my apartment-mates and I are a responsible group of guys who clean our apartment every Sunday. Maybe that's not true, but we definitely clean it at least once a month. Alright, the truth is we haven't technically "cleaned" the apartment yet this year, and I believe I used to have five roommates but one is now buried somewhere under old copies of *Sports Illustrated* and empty boxes of Domino's pizza.

The girls that live below us have a system for cleaning up. Each person is assigned a different area of the apartment to clean each week. However, I think our system of not cleaning at all is better because the girls are constantly getting in arguments over chores, while we guys have never fought about it.

Dave: Hey Matt, are those your nasty plates stacked on the couch?
Matt: Yep.
Dave: Okay, fair enough.

A bunch of guys living in an apartment together is

really just a battle to see who can clean up the least without dying of an infectious disease. We're each wondering, "Who's gonna' cave in first?" Instead of cleaning up, we will find ways to live in peaceful coexistence with the nastiness. If my feet start to stick to the kitchen floor, I'll wear shoes. If sewer rats set up camp in the pantry, we make friends with them, and sometimes they'll even help pay for groceries.

The reason each guy can't crack and clean something up is because if he does, he will permanently become "the guy that cleans." From then on he'll be *expected* to clean. Even if one guy spills motor oil all over the kitchen table, that guy will think, "Forget about it—Tony will clean that up. He always does." This will be the other guys' thinking even if Tony is the nastiest man alive and hasn't bathed for three years. Just because Tony took out the garbage that first time, he's "the guy that cleans."

There are essentially four main problem areas in my apartment that need desperate attention.

1. The Bathroom
2. The Trash Can/ Kitchen Area
3. The Bathroom
4. My Roommate

In my apartment we have an industrial size trash can that allows us to only have to empty the trash once a week. This does not change the fact that we empty the trash once a month. The trash tends to pile up until it begins consuming visitors to our apartment. Usually after there have been many fatalities, I come back to find that the trash is gone. The trash isn't gone because one of us took it out; it's because the trash becomes repulsed by the living conditions and goes to reside somewhere cleaner, such as a public dumpster.

The carpet in our common room has not been vacuumed in the traditional sense since MC Hammer had a career. For us "cleaning the carpet" entails kicking large chunks of food under the couch. The good thing about it is that if we're trapped in our apartment during some freak accident, we'll have at least a two month supply of food ground into the carpet. Our technique for cleaning dishes, on the other hand, is to leave them at various locations around the room and hope that eventually they'll get together and take a group bath.

Now on to the bathroom. To put it simply our bathroom could easily be used as a torture chamber to force enemy spies to reveal their secrets. If spies were locked in our bathroom, we would hear constant screams of, "The horrid stench is burning my nostrils" and "I just stepped on something squishy yet crusty!" Come to think of it, I find myself yelling that every morning.

I've also recently realized that our bathroom is growing hair. I don't know why or how, but our bathroom could be the spokesperson for Rogaine. We've basically stopped putting a bathmat down because the tile floor has grown its own. Besides, the formerly white bathmat has hardened into a solid brown slate anyway.

Well, I could go on longer but something under my desk is biting at my ankles.

Traumatic Memories and Mystery Meats

I think we can all agree that sometimes our lives get difficult. They seem to be spinning out of control, and nothing seems to be going right. It is during these times that we need a release; a way to relieve stress and realize that life's not so bad. One way is to watch *America's Funniest Home Videos* and laugh heartily every time an unsuspecting father gets nailed in the balls by his toddler (which is about every six seconds).

But sometimes that just doesn't do it anymore. And it is during those times I find the best solution is to think back to my most painful memories and be thankful that they're in the past. For me, nine out of ten of those painful memories occurred at the college cafeteria. Let's reminisce, shall we?

Eating in the cafeteria was an excruciating experience, a traumatic adventure and a complicated process all rolled neatly into a veggie wrap. If you weren't ready to devote a great deal of time and effort into food consumption, then the college cafeteria was not for you. It also wasn't for small children, pregnant women, pregnant men and most woodland creatures.

The cafeteria boasted five basic food groups that were supposed to be sampled at every meal. These groups were meats, breads, cereals, leftovers and ice cream. Having a serving from all five helped every student get the right amount of such vitamins and minerals as waffle iron. Waffle iron was scientifically proven to strengthen bones and cause a strong desire to wear plaid.

The first group, meats, was a very strange and confusing group. The reason humans eat meat actually goes back thousands of years. Before that time humans only ate plants, nuts, roots and gummy bears. One day a large man in overalls bit into cow for the first time. Needless to say, the cow kicked the man in the head (rendering him unconscious) but it was too late; mankind had gotten a taste for meat. As soon as the man could walk again, he resumed eating meat, but this time it was in the form of a pre-processed patty. In the years that followed people prepared meat in various forms, such as the whopper and the shepherd's pie. To this day no one is sure what is in the shepherd's pie, but my personal opinion is that this "pie" should have been kept out on the ranch with the shepherds instead of finding its way into my college cafeteria. Note for any vegetarians still in college: You too should have a serving from the meats group because most of the meats at college cafeterias contain no meat. Besides, the veggie-burgers are only meant for use as coasters.

The next group was breads. There's nothing funny about bread. It's a very serious matter. That's all I have to say about that.

In college the cereals group was enjoyed for all three meals of the day. Cereal was always easily accessible and well utilized. However when adding milk to your cereal you had to be on guard because for some reason beyond my understanding, the milk came out of tubes hooked up to a strange milk distribution contraption instead of the normal beverage taps. I guess it's so that we could feel like we were having the experience of actually milking a cow. Maybe the tubes were meant to resemble udders. I think they should have taken it a step further and just had cows in the cafeteria. We would have then been able to choose the cow we liked most (skim cow, two percent cow or chocolate cow). The cafeteria at my school allowed the students to make their own waffles. Why not milk their own cows?

The left-over group was an extremely significant group because it constituted eighty-five percent of what the cafeteria served. The general idea was "Yesterday's sausage is today's omelet mystery meat, and today's omelet mystery meat is tomorrow's fruit salad." That process continued in a giant cycle bigger than Water Gate, until the final line of leftovers was dried out and made into napkins. The left-over process was bigger and ran deeper than one could have ever conceived, and if for some reason you attempted to expose this process, you would have found yourself dealing with large, pushy men with names like, "Slippery Pete" and "Ox The Bull." How and why the leftovers cycle existed is just one of those questions that needs to remain unanswered, much like where the heck The Energizer Bunny is going. Is he lost? Why doesn't somebody help him? You get my point.

The ice cream group was central to the cafeteria as an institution. For some reason *everybody* wanted ice cream in great quantities. Many people seemed to wander up to the ice cream machine not knowing how they got there. All they knew was that they wanted ice cream. A lot of people started pumping the ice cream out so that it enveloped their cone and began to teeter over the edge. Nonetheless, they kept pumping until they had their own weight in ice cream stacked onto the over-burdened, structurally unsound cone and rainbow sprinkles were frantically evacuating. I'm convinced that if these people had their way, they would have stuck their faces under the pump and filled themselves with French Vanilla until it oozed out of their eye sockets.

In the confusion of college dining, it was easy to forget that the cafeteria was run by the hard working, highly skilled dining staff. And if you think back to those weird, tasteless meals, I'm quite certain you will realize that each one was served with a little slice of love. Thank you dining staff. Thank you.

7 Most Popular College Foods

1. Ramen Noodles
2. Old Beer
3. Hot Pockets (Ramen Noodle flavor)
4. Ravioli (cooked on a George Foreman Grill)
5. ~~Baked chicken breast in a light white wine sauce~~ Beer
6. Jell-O shots
7. Stuff found in the couch cushions a la beer

The Truth about Thomas Jefferson Revealed

I did, in fact, receive a degree from the University of Virginia, although they may deny it now. As a tribute to the founder of that great school, Thomas Jefferson, I would like to take a moment to review his life's achievements as seen through the eyes of someone who's making a lot of it up. This one's for you, Tommy J!

The year was 1812. Big, puffy white wigs were the latest fashion, and a young America was sitting back into a giant Lay-Z-Boy to enjoy a time of peace and some Doritos. Contrary to popular belief, 1812 was indeed a time of peace because the War of 1812 actually took place in 1816, but there were already neat things going on in 1816. So historians decided to attribute the war to the factually-barren year of 1812.

However, one thing important did occur in 1812 – it was the year that Thomas Jefferson decided to found a university. Although initially called Florida State University in hopes that it would have a good football team, the college eventually took on the name the University of Virginia.

So right now you're probably thinking, "Who is this Thomas Jefferson fellow you speak of?" Well, he was born in 1743 in Shadwell, Virginia. His parents expected great things from him right from the start, seeing as his picture was on U.S. currency. He could walk when he was only one year old, speak two languages at age two and was elected to the Virginia Assembly at four.

This early success took a toll on the young Jefferson because he couldn't live the normal life of a four-year-old. His friends rarely made the trek up to Monticello, little Thomas's estate, and even when they did, he was too busy.

Friend: Hey Tommy. Want to go play hopscotch?
Jefferson: I have to finish my homework, "A Summary View of the Rights of British America."
Friend: You never have time to play. I'm not gonna' vote for you in the next election.

Jefferson was soon a smart, young politician. Once a few Virginia Assembly terms were under his belt and a couple of

Continental Congress sessions were in his pants, Jefferson drafted the Declaration of Independence in 1776.

Just a few short years later Jefferson was elected Governor of Virginia with a platform based on the slogan, "We're bound to get it right one of these days!" During this time Jefferson watched as Cornwallis surrendered to George Washington in a heated bout of mud wrestling during the Revolutionary War. As governor, Jefferson's biggest contribution was changing Virginia's state motto to "Virginia is for lovers" from the original "Virginia is for road kill." With this kind of revolutionary thinking, it is no surprise that Jefferson was elected to Congress in 1783.

In 1787 Jefferson contributed greatly to the U.S. Constitution even though his idea of writing it in erasable pen was shot down (simply because nobody wanted to make the trip to 1987 to pick them up).

After a brief bout of vice-presidency in the 1790's, Jefferson was elected President of the United States. One of the highlights of his administration was the purchase of the Louisiana territory, which he found on sale at a small French boutique.

The key point of his second term as President came when he got sick of two guys named Lewis and Clark always hanging around the White House and sent them on an expedition out west. They ended up doing a service to all of America with their discovery of an exorbitant supply of prostitutes in Nevada. The end of Jefferson's presidency was basically a long rally in support of a bill that would have moved the White House to Nevada.

Jefferson retired to Monticello after the conclusion of his presidency. According to some accounts he did nothing but watch TV for several years (which was odd because television, of course, did not exist at that time).

In 1815 the Library of Congress bought much of Jefferson's extensive book collection from him at a yard sale.

Upon their return to Washington, employees at the Library of Congress discovered that Jefferson had charged them for the Louisiana territory as well as the books. After a bitter dispute in which Jefferson angrily asked, "How do I know you didn't walk out of here with the Louisiana territory?" he was forced to refund their money.

He got on with his life and founded Central College some time after the Egyptian pyramids were built and before *Seinfeld* went off the air. Central College became the University of Virginia one year before Jefferson died in 1826. (Some people claim that Jefferson did not die, but instead was kidnapped by alien dwarfs. There is very little evidence to support this claim except for a tiny silver shoe found at Monticello.)

Jefferson was a great man who left a frightening amount of legacy and tradition in his wake. He was a simple yet complex man. He was an aristocrat yet a common man. He liked grapes yet not grape Skittles. He was a stylish dresser yet often walked around his neighborhood in his underwear. He didn't drink alcohol, but he would get sloppy drunk off mouth wash.

Now that his history is a little more clear, we can remember him as he truly was (four feet tall, patch over one eye, right arm noticeably longer than the left, always wore lipstick).

A Gourmet Burrito Lightly Nuked in A Glucose-Free Saran Wrap Coating

I recently realized that the health craze now rules everything in our society. Everywhere you look there are gyms, or people working out in gyms, or people on their way to the gym, or home gyms, or guys named Jim, or guys named Jim who work out in gyms and own home gyms. You get the idea.

Everybody I know is watching their weight and watching each other's weight. When you go to the movies, you can't even ask for hot fudge on your popcorn without people looking at you funny. And people point at you when you're on the tread mill and happen to be eating a bacon cheeseburger with a side of chicken-friend steak. It's really gotten out of control.

But I must admit I've given in to the health insanity as well. I used to be on a diet, but it was great because it consisted of all-you-can-eat junk food, Pop-Tarts, and cheap pasta with sodas to drink. It was called "college."

Every student knows there are certain staples to the college diet, the most important one being ramen noodles. I'm pretty certain that if there were no ramen noodles, the majority of college students would die of starvation. You can almost see the two detectives walking through the deserted college town:

Rookie: It's sickening! There's nobody left alive. What could have possibly caused such a horrible tragedy?!
Veteran detective: Ramen noodles.
Rookie: What?
Veteran detective: They ran out of ramen. I've seen it all before. When will they learn?!!

Personally, I'm glad that college is based on microwave-ready dinners and ninety-nine cent hamburgers because I can't cook, and, more importantly, I hate to cook. I just can't convince myself that all the shopping, preparation, preheating, measuring, mixing, slicing, dicing, stirring, timing, baking, heating, grilling, frying, and serving is worth it. And even after I've done all that, my toast still comes out too spicy.

The truth is my cooking skills consist of remembering to take the wrapper off the microwaveable burrito. But I still consider myself a good cook because I have many friends who nuke the burrito with the plastic wrapper on and then complain it's too chewy. Plus, there are a countless number of people in this country who avoid cooking as actively as I do. (Actual number: four.)

One reason I avoid cooking is that even when I do cook, it doesn't come out right. For example, recently I got up the energy to cook a gourmet chicken dish with a light wine sauce, and despite all my time and effort, I forgot about the chicken and just got plastered off the wine.

I guess my disinterest in cooking stems from my mom's less-than-enthusiastic attitude towards it. Don't get me wrong, my mom does have some things she can cook well. I must say, her pecan pie is among the best there is, although you can gain close to three hundred pounds from one serving.

However, some of my mom's other cooking does not turn out so well. Once during my sophomore year of high school, she baked cookies for a class party, and they turned out to have the structural integrity of granite. I don't know how she did it, but these cookies could have withstood nuclear testing. In fact, when the students had a food fight, they ruled my mom's cookies off limits because they were afraid someone might get hurt. (This is all true by the way.) Then someone dropped one of the impenetrable balls of hardened dough out the third story window, and it didn't so much as dent.

There are basically two reasons my mom's cooking comes out wrong sometimes. First, I don't believe my mom has any sense of taste, so everything seems good to her. I think all adults lose their sense of taste as they get older. When you're little you can't stand the taste of things like mustard because they're too strong. Then, by your thirties you put mustard on everything because otherwise you can't taste it. And just a few short years after that, you have to set fire to your tongue just to know you're actually eating something.

The second reason my mom's not the best cook is that she's always on the go. So if she doesn't have an ingredient, she'll substitute whatever else is handy. If the recipe calls for creamed corn and she doesn't have any, she'll substitute corned beef. Or if an ice cream pie recipe calls for chocolate syrup, and we've run out, she'll instead use dog food.

I can't really blame her because I don't like devoting much time to cooking either. If, at the final stages of cooking a meal, I find out I don't have a crucial ingredient, I usually throw the unfinished dish at passing motorists. So obviously I've inherited some of my mother's traits.

But I am not bothered by my lack of cooking skills because cooking has plenty of drawbacks too. If you cook too much, you'll get addicted, and then your clothes start to stink and people don't want to be around you. Not to mention the possibility of lung cancer and emphysema. Wait, that's smoking I'm thinking about. Well, cooking is bad too.

GOURMET COLLEGE.

The Best Team Since Beer and Pretzels

Imagine a group of humans who live deep in the jungles of a far off country, such as Disney World. Now imagine that they know nothing of the civilized world. Sure, an occasional Disney Dollar has blown their way, but basically they don't know of civilization. Because they know so little of the rest of the world, they do crazy things like set their clocks forty-five minutes ahead, sleep on top of the covers on their beds with all their day-time clothes on and call their moms "Dude." Now try to imagine having one of these strange beings as a roommate. This seemingly ridiculous situation was my reality throughout college, except my roommate stemmed from the city of brotherly love instead of the city of animated love. Nino was his name. Nino was his game. And he had a plan to stick it to the man.

Although he may have been a little eccentric, he was not the nightmare roommate. I suppose it could have been worse, like if he had sat in the corner of the room waiting for me to return so he could jump at me with a pair of safety scissors and yell "Sic Semper Humor Columnists!" Luckily Nino was not like that; he only jumped at me with small pieces of pizza.

Like any college roommates, we had to deal with many frightening problems. The greatest of these problems of course being mold.

When Nino and I returned from one particular winter break we were abruptly confronted with the fact that mold had gotten extremely jiggy with some fruit that had been left in the refrigerator. We knew we had to launch a counter offensive, but before we could do that, we needed to watch a couple hours of television. Afterwards we tried to entice the mold out of the fridge, "Here Moldy, Moldy."

Didn't work.

We then tried reverse psychology, "Fine, we like having

mold in the fridge. I think it should just stay there because it would really bother us if it left."

Still didn't work.

We were out of ideas, and right when we were about to give up, the mold disappeared. It left a note which read, "You guys are the most pathetic people we have ever met, and we moved out because we didn't want to be seen associating with you. It was ruining our social life."

When we weren't doing something important, such as arguing about how wide to open the window (often compromising down to a thousandth of a centimeter), we were having top secret conversations concerning national security such as the following one (which is true).

Nino: Thphrunjrrye.
Me: What?
Nino: Thphrunjrrye.
Me: I have no idea what you just said.
Nino: Th-Phrun-Jr-Rye.
Me: Ohhhhhh. The furniture's dry. Thanks, I was wondering about that.
Nino: THE PHONE JUST RANG!
Me: Jeez, you don't need to yell.

Despite our differences, I think we worked very well together. We ranked right up there with some of the greatest teams in history such as Bonnie and Clyde, Scooby Doo and Shaggy, the 1972 Miami Dolphins, and beer and pretzels. An example of our excellent team work is the code we devised in the unlikely event that one of us had a girl in the room. The plan worked like this: If Nino had a girl in the room, and he asked me if I was going home next weekend, I was then supposed to exit the building and not come back for at least five minutes. We did notice that there was a problem with this system when Nino happened to be actually asking me if I was going home for the weekend. There was at least one instance in which Nino was in the room with only a protractor and some salsa, and he accidentally asked the secret question. With a little bit of a puzzled look, I immediately left the room.

We treated each other with a high level of respect which was equivalent to that of most wild oxen. As friends we took it upon ourselves to give useful criticism to each other when necessary. Some of the suggestions on self improvement included, "You smell," "Your music collection looks like it belongs to a twelve-year-old girl," "You look like you're in your second trimester," "Is it Spring already? Because I see a pansy" and "Okay, I'm gonna' need you to shut the hell up."

The wonderful thing about a good roommate is that memories are created that often last a lifetime. I have no doubt that in sixty years I will be surrounded by my grandchildren, and I will begin to tell a story. "College was some of the best years of my life. I think I lived alone. Wait, wait, never mind. I might have had a dog. I think I named it Nino . . ."

7 Ways to Frighten A New Roommate

1. Say, "Do you know how easily I could cut your toe nails while you're sleeping?"
2. Cut his toe nails while he's sleeping
3. Insist on sleeping with your head in the microwave and feet in the freezer
4. Put gophers in his underwear drawer
5. Replace all his shoes with cowboy boots
6. Replace all his shoes with cowboys
7. Yell "Boo!" really loud

A Not-So-Accurate History
of the University of Virginia

It is well known that the University of Virginia has enough history to fill several volumes of books and a pair of John Popper's boxer shorts. Such an immense amount of history is often hard for the average person to grasp, or at least store without heavy duty Tupperware.

I have condensed the important parts of UVA's history into an easy-to-swallow, hand-held column, which is partially untrue (and the other part is fabricated).

Our story begins in 1816 when Thomas Jefferson founded Central College. He soon changed the name because his friends continually made fun of him, "Hey Thomas, what's it the center of? Charlottesville? That sucks!" In 1818 the school became Jefferson's College of Interpretive Dance, later to be changed again to whatever it is now.

Several very interesting and comical things occurred during the construction of UVA, but in order to do those stories justice, I would need a large cast of puppets and two Italian men.

One interesting fact is that the first Board of Visitors consisted of Thomas Jefferson, James Monroe, Tito Jackson, an Irish wolfhound with only one eye, and a young, slender Fat Albert (then just called Albert).

During the early years, it became a tradition for the students to revolt every November twelfth (or some other specific day of the year) and go wild, firing blank rounds at the houses of professors. In 1840 two students, Joseph Semmes and Other Guy, were taking part in this ritual. Semmes masked his face with paint while Other Guy chose a rich, caramel sauce. Professor Davis, a much-loved (in more ways than one) member of faculty, wanted to put a stop to the misbehavior, so he disguised himself as a Doric column. When Semmes came by, Davis grabbed him and attempted to identify the student. Davis tried to rub the paint off, but it was apparent he would at least need some club soda. Semmes proceeded to shoot Davis in the stomach and groin with real bullets. (Although I would like to take credit for any groin jokes, I didn't make that part up.) The masked miscreants then fled to wash off the paint and caramel before it clogged their pores.

Davis received first aid from a group of extremely competent doctors who decided that he was not going to die. Just before Davis died two days later, he was requested to name his masked assailant but responded simply, "Trust honor, all of you. And then shoot the SOB's nads off." Despite popular belief, these were not Davis' last words. His true last words were, "Would you be a doll and fetch my bed pan?"

Other Guy was soon identified, and authorities went about making him name the second gunman on the grassy knoll. First they tried good cop – bad cop, then bad cop – bad cop, then good cop—ugly, fat, naked cop, then the construction worker from the Village People took a crack at it. When Other Guy finally named Semmes as the killer, people were outraged that he turned on his friend after only a few days of excruciating interrogation and questioned whether he knew anything about honor. So the UVA honor system was then created to stop lying, cheating, stealing and squealing on friends.

Another fascinating story is that of the fire in the Rotunda. The fire started in a corridor a short distance from the Rotunda sometime between noon on October 27, 1895 and the kickoff of the 1982 Super Bowl.

First students and professors tried a bucket brigade to stop the fire. However, at that time, just as today, alcohol ran like water at the University, and the fire fighters found that dumping Jack Daniels on the flames helped very little.

Students and professors soon got worried that the blaze would reach the Rotunda. They knew it would be tragic if the Rotunda burned down because streakers would not know where to stop, perhaps running naked until arrested at the

Canadian border. Meanwhile, one professor yelled, "We can get new students! Just save the books!" So men and women tried to save Jefferson's books by dumping them out the windows, knocking several students below unconscious.

Soon an excruciatingly smart man named Professor Echols did some very confusing, intricate physics equations resulting in the answer 23×10^{16}. Although positive he was correct, Echols had no idea what this number meant. He then remembered a common expression, "Always fight fire with heavy explosives." He obtained one hundred pounds of dynamite from the Dynamite Rental Room in Clemens Library and attempted to blow up the portico between the fire and the Rotunda. It wasn't enough, so Echols began hurling more dynamite and flammable-looking students onto the structure. The resulting explosion shattered every window in the Rotunda. At this point it is recorded that Jefferson actually rolled over in his grave and scratched his eyes out.

Despite Echols' extreme efforts to blow lots of things up, the fire eventually burnt down the Rotunda. When the Rotunda was rebuilt, the "furnace and oily rag room" was moved to a new location.

Between 1898 and 1969 nothing of interest happened at UVA to my recollection. However, in 1970 females were first admitted to the school. This forced the male students to change the traditional dress code from "coat and tie" to "coat and tie and pants."

Well, I think it is evident that UVA has an interesting and exciting past based on death and destruction. Jefferson probably never imagined that his school would become what it is today because if he had, he surely would have built a liquor store nearby.

An All-Inclusive Guide to Studying

During my numerous years in college (thirty-two to be exact), I learned a little something about studying. To sum it up briefly, I learned to avoid studying like it's a door to door salesman with a nasty, contagious rash and bad breath. (If you're married to someone like that, I mean it in the best possible way.)

The first step to studying is to go through your notebooks and highlight anything that's relevant. The reason it's important to highlight in your notebooks is so you know not to study the things you've doodled on the side of the page. For example, "don't forget to buy paper" or "I want to kick the professor in the face." Because if you don't highlight, you'll think that kicking the professor in the face is going to be on the final exam. Wouldn't that be great?

"23) Where do you want to kick the professor?
    a) the shin
    b) the ear
    c) the face
    d) all of the above"

You would be thinking, "Damn it, I should know this! I think it's 'the face,' but 'all of the above' sounds good too."

When studying, also beware of the temptation to study with a study group. Just know that there is no such thing as a study group. There may be groups that talk about how to study, or even stubby groups, but there is no group that actually studies. Study group conversation usually goes as follows:

"Let's study."
"Good idea. Who wants to get some candy with me?"
"I love those Swedish fish."

"What makes them Swedish anyway? Were their parents from Sweden?"

"Yeah, why does that candy have a regional background? There aren't any Yugoslavian Sour Patch Kids."

"That's candy racism! I'm too angry to study."

"Study what?"

I will now go over everything you will need to know to ace any college exam. My great lack of knowledge in most of these areas should make them surprisingly helpful.

History: Answer all questions with, "During that time period a boldly courageous man named *(fill in name of good guy)* made incredible advances in the area of human rights to the great dismay of *(fill in name of bad guy)*. It must also be noted that women were achieving their goals as well, seeing as their fearless leader *(name of good woman)* succeeded in kicking sexist America in the crotch. Meanwhile, our powerful and brave President *(name of President)* was defeating *(name of any country)* while still having time to sleep with *(name of woman)*, *(name of woman)*, and *(name of woman)*."

Philosophy: Begin all responses with either "Plato philosophized . . ." or "Niche extrapolated . . ." It doesn't matter what you say in the rest of the sentence as long as it starts in that manner. You will still get an A on the exam even if you put, "Plato philosophized that time was relative as long as Pepsi tasted better than Coke. Obviously Plato's thinking was ahead of his time."

English: For any question, make sure your response includes at least three mentions of Shakespeare in every sentence.

Hebrew: Act like you're choking – you'll probably be speaking fluently whether you know it or not.

Latin: Give a speech about how it's disrespectful to talk about a dead language.

Spanish: Bring in a Chihuahua to help you on the test because if there is anything we've learned from Taco Bell commercials, it's that Chihuahuas speak both Spanish and English fluently, and have a great sense of humor to boot.

Psychology: Respond "The writer of this question clearly has unconscious tendencies towards sexism which are subtly presented in the wording. These feelings most likely stem from a distrust of his or her father during childhood. I am greatly offended and refuse to answer any further questions until the writer gets past his or her denial and seeks psychiatric help."

Astronomy: For any question simply recite things that you remember from "Star Trek"; most of it's close enough. However, keep in mind the main thing that is not true is that every planet has an atmosphere exactly like earth's. In reality most planets have atmospheres that would either melt Captain Kirk's flesh into a puddle or freeze his bodily fluids completely solid within seconds.

Chemistry: You're on your own with that one.

Biology: Remember that 1980's movie "Inner Space?" That'll tell you everything you need to know.

Anthropology: Respond "I cannot answer this question because it depends on the meaning of the word 'the.' 'The' is a culturally loaded word which doesn't even exist in some Native American languages and in others refers to a type of mango. So until this word is more clearly defined, I cannot simply disregard the societal ambiguity inherent therein."

Math: On the exam explain that infinity equals zero, so dealing with any numbers in between is inconsequential and a waste of your finite amount of time on this planet.

Architecture: When in doubt, Frank Lloyd Wright designed it.

For all other subjects: Use a combination of the above answers.

I Want to Be Aquaman When I Grow Up

I remember when I first got to college, there was one thing my friends, family members, relatives and household pets always asked me – "What are you going to do with your life?" Everybody acts like the second you show up at college there is a person passing out life plans. This impression couldn't be further from the truth, unless of course by "life plans" they meant alcohol. In which case they are, in fact, correct.

In our society we're expected to find out what we want to be at a very young age. There is the omnipresent question of, "What do you want to be when you grow up?" Even in kindergarten, the crayon colors gave us a way to show what kind of occupation we were preparing for. At age six you might not have been ready for the Navy, but you knew you were on the right track because you were using the "navy blue" and "cadet blue" crayons. For the little chef, meaning the kid that would jam all his food into a ball and ask other kids to try it, there were plenty of colors to show his profession. He had "apricot," "melon," and even "cornflower." If he wanted to add a little attitude to his crayon recipes, there was also "wild strawberry," and "atomic tangerine."

For the six-year-olds looking into a career in marine biology, there was "sea green" and "aquamarine." For toddlers having trouble with their love life, "bittersweet" was a good choice. This could be used for those times when rainbow colors just didn't fit the mood. Aspiring carpenters usually used the manly, carpentry-oriented colors such as "brick-red," "burnt sienna," and "rusty red." For those of you who were preparing to be a lumberjack at age six, there was "pine green," "jungle green," "forest green," "green yellow" and "yellow green." How many preschoolers really differentiated between the "green yellow" and the "yellow green" anyway?

"Billy, cou-cou-could you hand me the g-g-green yellow, please? . . . Thanks . . . WHAT THE HELL IS THIS—THE YELLOW GREEN?!! I'M TRYING TO CREATE A WORK OF ART HERE, AND YOU HAND ME THE YELLOW GREEN?!! I'M WORKING WITH IDIOTS!!"

However, when I was about four, I decided that I wanted to be either Aquaman or a crocodile. To my dismay, I later found out that those occupational choices were neither physically nor technologically possible, but I maintain high hopes.

There was a lot of pressure for me to figure out my life's direction back in college because everybody around me already knew where their lives were headed. My roommate wanted to be an architect, my older brother planned to be a lawyer and my younger brother was an aspiring rodeo clown of some sort.

So with everybody around me mapping out promising futures, I figured that I should start thinking about mine, or at least deciding whether I should spend my Thursday nights watching "When Good Times Go Bad" or "When Good People Get Eaten." The truth is that back then my life was jam-packed with tough decisions. Psychology or English major? Get a job or watch TV? Lettuce or tomato? And then, right when I thought those questions were hard enough, I remembered the one possibility that continues to trouble me to this very day: I could get both lettuce *and* tomato.

So, I charted my life out in much the same way that a blind, drunken sailor avoids rocks: After each devastating collision, I changed direction. "Arrr, matie. We're headed for medical school. Wait, is that seven years of school and hard work up ahead? Hard to starboard! Hard to starboard! Set a new course for English major."

7 Stress Relievers

1. Listening to a tape of ocean sounds
2. Yelling profanities
3. Closing your head in a car door
4. Closing someone else's head in a car door
5. Yoga completely nude in the middle of a library
6. Cracking your knuckles
7. Just plain crack

2

Childhood

The Carefree Days of Childhood
—Thank God They're Over

Recently I was reminiscing about the wonderful times I had during my elementary and middle school days. Those were carefree and fun-loving times, weren't they? Wait, were they? No, I hated elementary and middle school.

Back then, every day was a battle to keep your dignity, put up with tyrannical teachers, find something edible in the cafeteria, not get picked last in kick ball and not be named the smelly kid (because the smelly kid always got picked last in kick ball).

Yet the true anguish came from the teachers. Nearly every teacher was either clinically insane or extremely angry at life. Just think about the teachers you had. I bet you had at least three that refused to let you use the bathroom at any point during class. I can't understand how these teachers slept each night knowing they nearly made a ten-year-old's bladder explode. And this came from men and women that had very little bladder control of their own.

Yet I'm sure you had crazier teachers than that. I had one

who announced to the class, "Children, it's that time of year when you need to shower every day. Charles needs to sit outside because he stinks." Unfortunately for Charles, I'm not making this up.

Even if the teacher wasn't mean, each one had some sort of obsession. At various times I had teachers who were obsessed with butterflies, bumble bees, cats, Van Gogh, Patrick Swaze, and Michael Jordan. (Once again, all of this is true.) I had another teacher who was terrified of the Tin Man from "The Wizard of Oz." And we all had – and perhaps still have – the teacher who read sex into everything. "Class, you have to look at the metaphorical meaning to clearly see that this book is about nothing but sleazy, dirty, hardcore, animal sex. Don't you see that when the Grinch steals 'Christmas,' he's really stealing the town's virginity? You're never going to get through second grade at this rate!"

Most of us also had that certain teacher we were smarter than, and he or she didn't like it too much. Whenever you would ask an intelligent question, he or she would answer, "We're not getting into that in this class. To answer that we would need concepts that I don't want to get into right now." I wanted to say, "What is all this 'don't want to get into' crap? It's not an ugly pair of pants." And what the teacher really wanted to say was, "How the hell am I supposed to know the answer? Listen, I barely got into college, I drank my way through it and I thought I was majoring in psychology. But when I woke up, it said 'education' on my diploma. So unless the answer is in the damn teacher's guide, I don't want to get into it!"

But of course teachers couldn't say things like that because they didn't want to get fired. In fact, the best days in middle school were the days when the principal would come to evaluate your teacher during class. Those days were great because the teacher would try to act like she was doing the best job in the world, and this was the students' chance to mess with her. For example, you could start taking your clothes off, and when your teacher asked what the hell you were doing, you could say, "But Mrs. Fielding, yesterday you encouraged us to take our clothes off." (That is assuming your teacher's name was Mrs. Fielding because otherwise it would be quite awkward.) Or you could just raise your hand, "Mr. Garrett, my mom doesn't want you to give us crack anymore." I never saw Mr. Garrett again.

But let's not forget about the gym teachers. Those strong, stoic, motivational men and women who faithfully and selflessly taught us everything they had to offer about pain and anguish. From their lofty lawn chairs on the sidelines they put in hour after hour of hard work in order to change us from young boys and girls with no concept of self-control to grown men and women with no concept of dignity, pride or self-respect.

Gym teachers were usually both insane and highly unintelligent. This is never a good combination around children. The male gym teachers were generally horny old men who called each other "coach" as if it was a prefix with as much respect associated to it as "doctor." However, if "doctor" is a reference to a person's completion of medical school, I think "coach" is a reference to a person's completion of an entire keg of beer by themselves one night when they were in their mid-twenties.

On the other hand, the female gym teachers thought they were coaches for the East German Olympic team. They would make you run laps and give you a B in the class simply because you forgot your gym shorts. This came from women who probably once drove home with the wrong child after a trip to Disney World and then played it off by raising the new kid as their own.

The coaches' die hard commitment to making children run until one of each kid's lungs exploded seemed hypocritical considering the fact that most of these coaches needed to take a ten minute rest to catch their breath after checking attendance. I certainly can't recall a coach that was even close to being in shape unless that meant in the shape of a Jell-O mold. The only reason gym teachers inspired us to work hard was because none of us wanted to end up like them.

Okay, this is the part of the column in which I apologize to any teachers or coaches I've offended. I know that not every teacher is evil and not every gym teacher is fat, but stereotypes are so much fun, aren't they? So if you're a wonderful teacher or even a mediocre coach, then more power to you. Just remember one thing – let the poor kids go to the bathroom!

Caring and Scaring Go Hand in Hand

For anybody out there looking for a job, I can sympathize with your frustration. It's not easy to find normal, steady jobs anymore (I don't think there's an available mime or pimp position left in the nation.) I strongly recommend being a camp counselor.

Taking care of toddlers at a day camp is non-stop excitement, basically because most children stop taking their Ritalin over the summer. As a counselor you'll be able to kick off your shoes, let your hair down and enjoy nature. However, make sure not to literally kick off your shoes and let your hair down or you'll enjoy Lyme Disease and leeches.

The reason I so highly recommend this job is because a couple years ago I was a camp counselor, and now, I want others to go through the same painfully traumatic experience I did. Maybe I can further persuade you by telling you of the incredibly fulfilling experiences I had on the first day of camp.

It was hell before I even got on the camp grounds. On the bus ride to the camp one five-year-old was doing some sort of dance, which resembled the Macarena. When I asked him where he got his moves, he informed me that he "really had to pee" (technical terminology). He requested that I let him pee out the window of the bus. Although I did entertain the idea of *tossing him* out the window, I didn't think relieving himself would be appreciated by the children in the back of the bus getting soaked by the reentry spray. Luckily, the kid survived the trip without any noticeable bladder explosion.

Once at the camp, some other counselors and I took the fifteen kindergartners down to the lake. At the lake I learned the first of several important rules of the kiddy world: Small children don't care or give any thought to the consequences of their actions. One little boy, we'll call "Lucifer," immediately ran into the water up to his knees. He gave no thought to the fact that he would be wearing wet, muddy shoes for the rest of the day. Because it would have been cruel to make him walk around barefoot, we simply tied him to a hand truck like in *Silence of the Lambs*.

Next, we had to take the children to the pool. In the changing room I learned rule number two of their world: Five-year-olds see clothing as unnecessary and restraining. Clothes are just holding them back. Once they got naked, they ran around the changing room like fifteen grasshoppers in a small jar—just jumping around happily and banging their heads into the walls.

After bribing the children with the promise of more naked time later, we got them all to put on some sort of cloth that covered between the waste and knees. Rule number three was then learned: If an adult makes a rule, a child with an IQ of fifty can find at least 3,267 ways around it.

For example, let's consider the rule "Don't get in the pool." Simple enough. First, the kids will stick every body part possible in the water without being arguably "in the pool." Next, they will realize that you said "don't *get* in the pool," not "don't *be* in the pool." Therefore they'll *accidentally* fall in the pool, technically not *getting* in. However, since there is no rule against *being* in the pool, they will remain in the water. Finally, the genius kid in the group (there's always a genius kid) will find a way to evaporate the pool water, transport it over to his body and then condense it again.

Once free swim got under way, it was basically two hundred kids running around like the characters in *Lord of The Flies* high off Red Bull. One of the children's favorite games was to see who could run fastest around the sign that read, "Do Not Run."

After swim time was over, it was back to the changing room for more five-year-old naked time, which had quickly become the children's favorite time of day. Kids from other groups would sell periods of their naked time on the black market. You could hear deals going down around the camp, "I'll give you five minutes of my naked time for your juice box."

Rule four: When kids want food, they expect to get it. Luckily it was snack time. Yet, just because there is a time designated for snacking does not mean the camp had remembered to buy food. So, I just told the kids the truth. I told them that their mommies had worked in cooperation with several boogiemen to steal and devour the snacks. The kids didn't understand except for a few who wet themselves.

Next rule: Small children want to be carried—everywhere. And kids are like dogs when it comes to being carried—they always mark their territory. Some just smear mud on your shirt. Others leave behind gum, bite marks, scratch marks, dog doo, kid doo, a wet spot, drool, hair or fourteen-legged creatures.

Thankfully, we had arts and crafts next. The children finally stopped whining about lunch because they ingested enough paint and Elmer's Glue to tide them over.

At lunchtime I learned rule number six: Kids like jelly and juice; bees like jelly and juice; kids hate bees; bees can sting. Lunch consisted of bees chasing screaming five-year-olds around the camp. Then, when the bees fell to the ground with laughter, the kids hunted them down and threw rocks at them. The rocks were just enough to unite the entire bee community against the toddlers. What I witnessed that day was, I believe, more intense than the battle of Gettysburg.

On the front line, half the children swung sticks at the bees while a second line of kids threw rocks, food and each other at the flying insects. Initially the kids successfully confused the bees into retreat. However, the bees launched a counter offensive using guerrilla warfare. Five-year-olds were dropping left and right, and the bees triumphed. Afterward, we took the whole group to bathe in calamine lotion, and then we finally sent them home.

I hope I've convinced you that childcare is a fun-filled, high-energy opportunity that you should look into. If you'll excuse me, I need to go apply for a telemarketing position.

7 Rejected Children's Books

1. The Cat in The Casserole
2. The Hairy Potter
3. Is That a Wocket in Your Pocket or Are You Just Happy to See Me?
4. Green Eggs and Stan
5. How the Grinch Explained The Amortization of Intangible Business Assets
6. Old MacDonald Had A Root Canal
7. One Fish, Done Fish, Red Fish, Dead Fish: Let's Eat!

Elementary Water Torture

Seeing as it is summer time, I have received many letters from worried readers asking questions like, "Why haven't I seen anything about swimming pools?" and "Less funny, more swimmy!" Well, since I'm a man of the people, I will write a column about swimming pools in order to satisfy the desires of these readers who do not technically exist.

The house I grew up in actually did have a swimming pool. Most of you are probably thinking, "Wow, a pool must have been great when you were younger. All your friends coming over, wild pool parties, naked chicks." Well, that's what I thought too, but it didn't happen. There were few friends coming over, no wild parties, and certainly no naked chicks. At least not that didn't charge fifty dollars an hour.

You have to realize that past the age of six, kids and adults don't want to go swimming for recreational purposes. Adults basically only go swimming when pushed into a body of water by their obnoxious, attention-starved friend, Rob, who thinks it's hilarious to push people in the water with all their clothes on. As you can see, this is not the makings of a wild pool party.

Over the years my family had various "pool parties," and people would come, stand around the pool, size it up, talk about how great it must be to have a pool in your back yard, and talk about how nice it is that they don't have to actually get in the water.

It didn't help that our pool just happened to have the climate of Boston in February. For some reason our pool's temperature always has hovered around thirty-two, maybe thirty-three degrees. However, this came in handy on those sweltering summer days when we could walk up to the pool while sweating profusely and think, "Hey, at least I'm not in the pool."

In order to raise the pool's pathetically low overall fun rating, we went out and bought an assortment of inflatable devices, some arriving at our door in unmarked brown bags. The boxes to these inflatable rafts, tubes and animals all had pictures of incredibly happy people enjoying some sort of inflatable utopia. My brother and I would spend our summer afternoons attempting to inflate these monstrous rafts until at least one of us passed out.

We've also had chronic problems keeping our pool blue. That doesn't sound like it should be that difficult, sort of like keeping President Bush's verbal SAT score low. Well, we screwed it up somehow. Our pool seems to strongly prefer the color "nasty green" over the more popular "crystal-clear-with-a-light-blue-tint," which can be seen on every pool or hotel brochure ever made. Once the green tint consumes the entire pool, the pool begins to look more like the fishing hole out behind Uncle Jimbo's house, which is also a great place to swim as long as you keep an eye out for leeches and copperhead snakes.

The only thing worse than swimming in a green pool is being on a swim team. My mother insisted that I be on the swim team for at least two summers. It was possibly the most horrifying experience of my life.

Although I was young, I still was one of the worst swimmers ever to hit the water. I spent a great deal of my heroic swimming career tangled in lane lines. I couldn't bare waiting on those little benches and wearing a bathing suit that if seen in a movie, would result in an NC-17 rating. All the swimmers sat there, terrified and cold, anticipating a chance to avoid drowning while hundreds of excited parents thought to themselves, "Why don't they sell beer at these things?"

Eventually we got our turn up on the blocks, practically wetting ourselves (or maybe that was just me), as we prepared to dive into the water. I believe my pre-race mental attitude was, "Please don't let me drown. Please God, don't let me get eighth place. Just let me beat one kid. Let one poor kid be more pathetic than I am. That's all I ask."

Did I mention that my father set swimming records at the University of Florida? As you can tell, I planned on following in his footsteps.

During these swim meets, if any one of us false started and didn't know it, the officials would lower a line of string into the pool to stop us from swimming. That was by far the most exciting time of my life. When they lowered that line down, and I had no idea I had false started, I thought to myself, "Oh God! There's a string in a water! Lord, why dost thou spite me?! I must keep swimming! I'm getting tangled in this line of death! Not only will I lose the race and my last shred of dignity, I'm not going to make it out alive!" Finally, I lifted up my head to see a hundred people staring at me while the other swimmers still stood up on the blocks, now wetting themselves out of laughter. And on top of all this, I was forced to get back on the blocks and do it again when what I really wanted was to go home, have some milk and cookies and get in a warm bath with a toaster.

One good thing did come out of my glorious time on the swim team – it made the time in my own ice-cold green pool seem like a relaxing, tropical paradise.

3
Jobs

Summer Job Found to Be Moving Experience, Lame Pun Ruins Title

A few summers ago I was a professional mover. When I took this job for one day to help out my friend's uncle, I thought it had something to do with learning dance moves—I was mistaken. The only dancing a professional mover does is when he or she drops a three hundred and fifty pound refrigerator on his or her toe. Actually I took the job as a learning experience. I wanted to experience working hard all day, pressing my body to the limit and the incredible pain of pulling one's groin.

We started out that morning by carrying boxes of Christmas decorations down from a woman's attic. It really didn't seem that tough, and besides, Christmas decorations are fun. However, Christmas decorations led to Halloween decorations, which led to Thanksgiving decorations, which led to a two-ton sofa (adorned with Christmas decorations). My friend and I carried the sofa down the stairs with half of the weight on his legs and the other half on muscles I hadn't used since I pulled myself out of the womb. These muscles sent a message to my brain that read, "We're not for use. Aesthetic purposes only!" My brain quickly responded, "Don't look at me. I don't want to be here. I'd rather be home watching *The Price Is Right*." This helped very little, and the muscles then dropped the couch on my feet and ankles.

Here's a question: Why do you move stuff? You move it so that you can have it in a location where it better suits your needs. Why do you move somebody else's stuff? Wise men have puzzled over this question for centuries. There is no good answer to this question, and that was my main problem with working as a mover.

I would look at the heavy, awkward box that was meant to be transported from it's current location to a location several miles away, and I would think to myself, "I have no desire to move this box. It has no desire to be moved that I can see. It won't help me in any way to have this box anywhere other than in its current location. And once it's moved I won't be any better off." At this point I reported to my boss that the box, my muscles and I had agreed to leave the box where it was. My boss then threw an even heavier, more awkward box into my hands and sent me down the stairs.

As the day dragged on I realized that there is one phrase in moving that seems to come up over and over again. It's often useful to yell this phrase to fellow movers and bewildered spectators. The phrase is, "It won't fit!" There are two rules that go along with this phrase:

1. The house being moved out of will have doorways that are just barely big enough to move everything out.

2. The new house will have doorways approximately two inches narrower.

This universal law was actually discovered by Sir Isaac Newton one day while he was sitting under an apple tree and a grandfather clock fell on his head. Despite this law of moving, a good mover will be able to carefully widen the doorways by scraping all of the paint off the door frames with a bureau that is worth more than his or her life. I actually had little problem with the corners of objects scraping along the walls because I was lucky enough to have my fingers accidentally caught in between every time an extremely heavy object careened into a wall.

Here's some other interesting things that happened as the day went by:

- The boss got upset when I rode a big screen TV down the stairs.
- We spent thirty minutes trying to find a child that I had accidentally packed up.
- I impressed the entire moving crew by carrying a bookcase down a flight of stairs with most of its weight on my big toe.
- While carrying a China hutch, a strange muscle popped out of my shoulder. I put it in the truck with the other stuff.

Two purple finger nails and three sweat rags later, I was finished—the job complete, the damage done. I got paid forty-five dollars for the day. That works out to twenty-seven cents per strained or mutilated muscle.

Despite the hardship, I worked for the moving company again over winter break. This time we worked right after the city had been hit by an ice storm. If you haven't had a chance to watch movers on ice, it's a great spectator sport. In fact I hear ice moving may become an Olympic sport in the near future along with weightlifting on roller skates. Ice moving consists of strapping a couch to the back of a mover and then sending them down an icy slope. If this sport catches on, there also are plans for a refrigerator luge.

Being a professional mover is a tough job. Personally, I would rather have a desk job—one in which I sit at the desk instead of the desk sitting on me.

What The Customer Doesn't Know Can't Hurt The Employee

When I was seventeen my parents first decided they wanted me to get a job. They presented the idea to me like this:

Parents: You need to start working.
Me: I am working. Right now I'm working on the most efficient way to get the white stuff out of the middle of an Oreo.
Dad: Well done. Carry on, and brief me on your findings later.
Mom: No Lee, you need to get a job.
Dad: Honey, can't you see the boy is working? Don't bother him.
Mom: Lee, I'm serious.
Me: No hablo ingles.
Mom: Are you listening?
Dad: Honey, can't you see the boy doesn't speak English? You're probably frightening him.

Well, much to my dismay I ended up having to get a job. I rejected a normal job like tarot card reader or bearded woman in a freak show and decided to work in the pro shop at a local tennis club. I was taught the job over a two hour time period during which I only learned how to play Tetris on the computer. Once I got to the other side of the counter, I realized that employees don't know any more than the customers. They came to me for answers as if I was Alex Trebek, but, like *Jeopardy!*, I ended up answering in the form of a question, such as, "Why are you asking me??" Actually, the key to being a "good" employee is to sound like you know what you're talking about even though you never do.

What Employee Says	*What Employee Thinks*
Let me get back to you on that.	Damned if I know.
We don't have any in stock right now.	Where the hell did I put those?
Yes, that's correct.	Damned if I know.
Our computers are down at the moment.	I can't interrupt my solitaire game.
This racket is great for junior players.	Damned if I know.

As Pro Shop Guy (my official title), I had to be a good sales person as well as a good Tetris player. The pro shop sells such items as tennis rackets, tennis bags and tiny tennis shorts that when worn seem to shout out, "I like those of the same gender." Here are some examples of my excellent sales techniques.

Customer #1: I'd like a size six women's shoe.
Me: (realizing we only have size nine in stock) You're actually going to want a size nine
because this brand of shoe tends to shrink in the wash.
Customer #2: I was going to buy this racket, but it appears the frame is cracked in several places.
Me: Well, that is the newest advancement in frame technology. The "cracks" as you ignorantly called them, allow for a slingshot effect as the ball hits the racket. In fact, I'm going to have to charge you extra for those cracks.

One of the toughest parts of my meaningless job was trying to stop the club members from taking advantage of my incredible lack of knowledge when it came to anything and everything pertaining to my job. People were always trying to get court reservations before the designated time. They just didn't realize that I am a man of strong moral character and would, under no circumstances, give away an illegal reservation without a significant bribe.

Honestly, manning the pro shop is a very important job. It serves as the communication and organizational center for a Colombian drug cartel that operates out of the storage room. And hundreds of people rely on the pro shop to be ready and operative if they need a rag to wipe off whatever is stuck to their shoe. When I say "hundreds," I mean eight. Plus, if any club member should ever need a can of balls, a racket re-strung, a court reservation or tennis apparel, the pro shop is there to give them the name of someone who might be able to help.

The pro shop is not just any meaningless, overstaffed department. Don't kid yourself. It's a meaningless, over-staffed department that wreaks of goat milk due to a strange mishap by UPS. The pro shop is also the office and bathing area of high-paid professional tennis instructors, and me – The Pro Shop Guy! To the pro shop, Robin!

4

Sports

Kayaking Includes Fun on The Water, Poisonous Snakes

If you're looking for something remotely exciting to do over your weekend, try kayaking, but don't be mislead by the name as I was. Kayaking actually has nothing to do with yaks, which I found extremely disappointing.

The kayaking trip my girlfriend and I went on recently wasn't the "exciting, thrill-of-a-lifetime, crazy rapids, hit your head against a rock, and hope the authorities find your bloated body" kind of trip. Instead it was the "slow-going, paddle down a man-made canal, and look at grass" kind of trip.

We began our journey by getting comfortable with our kayaks. First, our guide went over simple paddling instructions such as, "remember to hold your paddles with both hands" and "try not to club the person sitting in front of you in the back of their head with your paddle." Up until that point, I had thought the goal of kayaking was to club the person sitting in front of you in the back of their head with your paddle.

I quickly began to feel defeated by this seemingly impossible sport because I was paddling hard but getting nowhere.

At this point, our guide informed us that we would soon get the opportunity to try kayaking in the water as opposed to on land. Once in the water, I found kayaking a great deal easier.

Our guide was a well-informed gentleman who had apparently been hit in the head by the paddles of confused beginners a few too many times. He was extremely upbeat about everything. "Anybody allergic to poison ivy? Well, there's a great deal of it on the bank of the canal, and I put a little bit in your kayaks for you to look at! Also, this water might be fun to swim in if certain kinds of plants didn't release toxins into it! By the way, try not to tip your kayak, but it might be fun to splash each other if it gets a little hot!!"

The guided kayaking trip that we signed up for was supposed to be a combination of kayaking and animal watching. However, apparently nobody told the animals about the trip, and they, for the most part, did not show up.

The grass, on the other hand, showed up in full force for the event. This was not your average, friendly, putting green grass. The grass, which seemed to have imperial control over the canal, was extremely sharp and painful. In fact, (I'm not making this up) our guide told us that in the past Native Americans used these grass blades to give themselves tattoos. I tried to avoid the ferocious greenery but accidentally brushed against it, resulting in a tattoo on my arm of Bob Dole wearing only a sombrero. Who would've thought a relative of the Chia Pet could be so evil? (I mean the grass is a relative of the Chia Pet, not Bob Dole.)

The highlight of the trip came when my girlfriend and I spotted a stick that seemed to be traversing across the canal at an impressive speed. We found it hard to believe that a four foot piece of wood, in a small canal, would be in such a hurry. Then it occurred to us that the object was not a stick at all but instead a full-grown hippopotamus. We were wrong though, and our guide informed us that it was a water moccasin, a type of poisonous snake, and although it was capable of killing us and everyone we cared about, it would most likely leave us alone. He also told us that if we respect a snake's territory, it will respect ours.

I wanted to know whether this policy had been conveyed to the snakes. Are we really sure the snakes understand? Did we send a representative to discuss it with them? When a snake falls from a tree and clamps on to my skull, am I going to be able to say, "Whoa, buddy. What do you think you're doing? Haven't you heard of The Human – Snake Agreement of 1982?" Is the snake going to respond, "Oh, you're right. You've got me on that one. I never did like that policy. I guess I should take it up with my local congressman. Sorry about that." If this is not the case, then we don't really have an understanding at all, do we?

Looking back on the trip, it was a lot of fun until that part at the end when the nocturnal killer mosquitoes came out by the hundreds and tore our flesh off. Other than that, it was great, and girls find the tattoo of naked Bob Dole sexy.

7 Things You Don't Want to Hear Your Guide Say on A Kayaking Trip

1. Hey, I'd be worried too if I had me as a guide
2. Don't worry. That type of snake can't swim . . . unless it's really hungry
3. (mumbling angrily to himself) I'll show my boss who isn't fit to be a guide
4. Okay, is everyone ready to paddle really fast past the rhinos?
5. There's nobody for miles – nobody to hear you yelling . . . I mean paddling, nobody to hear you paddling
6. Damn it! Does anyone know which way is west?
7. You don't have to be faster than the school of piranha, you just have to be faster than someone else in our group

Try Not to Hit Me in The Pommel Horse

I watched a lot of the summer Olympics in Sydney on television, and I think we can all agree that the opening ceremonies to the Olympics are always a little strange. From what I gathered this past summer, either those ceremonies were thought up by ex-hippies having LSD flashbacks or while I was watching it, I was having an LSD flashback. There were people flying from the rafters, puppeteers who had a tad too much heroin before the show, and about a million children of varying ethnicity dressed up like butterflies and fish with thyroid conditions.

Yet most of the sports at the Olympics are just as unusual. Who invented some of these gymnastics events, such as the pommel horse? "We'll have this thing that looks a little like a mechanical bull, we'll nail a couple of handles on it, and we'll see what these guys can do with that." We should spice the event up by making the pommel horse move like a mechanical bull. "Blaine Wilson of the United States has begun his routine. Let's see how he handles the bucking back and forth. He looks a bit disoriented. Oh! The pommel horse tossed him five feet into the air and he landed face-first into the parallel bars. But he's got the time to beat with 4.8 seconds."

I can't stand the judging in the gymnastics at the Olympics. The gymnastics is usually little fourteen-year-old girls flying through the air, doing triple back flips. Then they finally land on the mat at the end, and the announcer always says, "Ohhh, she moved her left pinky toe as she landed! She has let down her entire nation. Chances are she'll be disowned when she returns home, and her whole community will beat her with saplings and then chase her away into the jungle! What a pity!" Can't we give these little girls some credit for defying gravity and nearly killing themselves?

What we need to do is allow some average people to compete in the gymnastics events so these girls would feel good about themselves. "Well folks, as you just saw, Hasing from China took a half step to the left, quite possibly ruining China's hopes for a medal. But next up on the floor exercise for the USA—Davie from Minnesota. Davie is forty-two years old, he weighs three hundred and twelve pounds, and up until today he thought gymnastics had something to do with the Air and Space Program. Let's see what Davie can come up with. He has started out with a summersault. And another summersault. The judges might look down upon this excessive use of summersaults. Wait, he stood up. Looks like he's preparing for a double two and a half. No, it's another summersault. And to finish up, he's attempting a cart-wheel, . . . but it's ill-fated! He came down hard on his head! He just couldn't loft that big stomach into the air. This is not going to help USA's overall score."

I don't like watching men's swimming either because it looks like a white-supremacist pool party, though I'm pretty sure most skin-heads don't know how to swim. And even if they did, I don't think they would wear those skin-tight Speedo bathing suits.

How humiliating is that for those swimmers? You're on television across the entire world, and all you're wearing is tighty-whiteys. I think that's why those guys are swimming so fast. It's because they don't want people to see them. You strap a tiny bathing suit on me and put me on international television, I'd set some world records too. I feel bad for the swimmers. Imagine having to explain to the entire civilized world, "The water was cold. There was shrinkage."

It's insane that these guys shave their entire bodies so they'll go faster. I don't want to be involved in any sport in which my body hair plays a crucial role in the outcome. The announcers are like, "Oh, that's too bad. He would have set a world record, but he forgot to shave his arm pits."

My favorite recent development in the Olympics was the U.S. basketball Dream Teams. There's nothing like taking the best basketball players in the world and putting them up against a third world country to display a good old-fashioned American ass-whooping. It does seem a little unfair, though. Kevin Garnet can have three Lithuanians on his shoulders and still put the ball between his legs and dunk it.

I think the U.S. basketball coach has the easiest job. "Alright men, winning by forty points yesterday was pathetic! I've never seen such a group of pansies in my life! Today I want us up by sixty at the half. And Alonzo, thirty-six points in yesterday's game? What the hell kind of half-assed effort is that??"

Well, I suppose track coaches have it pretty easy too. "This time Marion, I want you to try going faster. The jogging approach just isn't doing it for us. So right when that gun goes off, I want you to think, 'Go fast!'"

The decathlon has always confused me, too. I can never come up with all ten sports that are involved. There's running, hurdles, long jump, javelin, shot put, high jump, . . . um . . . shimmy up a pole, pie eating contest, . . . maybe . . . log flume, and . . . catch a greased pig, right? Well, that's what it should be.

Basically, the Olympics needs to make some changes, and I'm going to be the man to initiate them. At the next Olympics if you see a three hundred pound man competing in the women's gymnastics, you'll know we're making progress.

Fun with SkiiiiiAAAA!

During spring break a few years ago, while my fellow college students were having the time of their lives in exotic locations where the local dress code is nothing but sand, I was in Colorado trying to kill myself. I mean, learning to ski.

Skiing consists of strapping an extremely slick piece of material to each foot and hurling yourself down an icy mountain while grasping sharp metal poles in your hands. I think this activity is actually number two in *Top 10 Activities Designed To Kill Both Participants and Innocent Bystanders*; the number one activity being drunk swing dancing with chainsaws on a tightrope. And don't worry, while skiing, if you don't kill or maim yourself on your first trip down the mountain, you can get back up and do it repeatedly until someone at least swallows a couple teeth.

In order to go skiing in twenty-degree weather, you have to begin by putting on every piece of clothing you have ever owned, including those lame T-shirts you haven't worn in ten years that say things like, "I'm Not Overweight – This T-shirt Adds 30 Pounds" and "If You Can't Stand The Heat, Get Off Your Asphalt!"

I knew I would be bad at skiing right away. I couldn't even figure out how to carry my skis correctly much less go down a mountain on them. When I got on the shuttle to the ski lift, I didn't know what to do with my skis. So I carefully placed them in the eye of the person behind me. He wasn't too pleased.

After I was locked into my skis until death did we part, I had to get on the ski lift. For inexperienced skiers mistakes on the lifts inevitably occur. For example, you might fall while you're getting off and cause the lift operator to stop the entire lift. You will then crawl out of the way, leaving your dignity in a puddle behind you while hundreds of skiers, stuck on the stationary lift, will shout encouraging words like, "When I get down from here, I'm gonna' stab you in the crotch with my pole!" However, a mistake on the lift could be something more insignificant, such as a thirty-foot fall to your icy death. But don't worry, that only happens to two or three people . . . per year . . . per ski resort.

The toughest thing about being an adult who is just learning how to ski is that you have to watch a myriad of toddlers speed by you on the slopes. I don't know how these kids learned to ski so young. They can't even eat solid food yet, but they can nail the moguls. On several instances I was sitting on my ass after a fall, and some infant skied up to me and tried to give me advice on how to ski. But the kids weren't even old enough to talk yet. They'd say things like, "Yuz, yuz, gotta' get, get go, yuz slippidy da boom."

I'd respond, "Thanks kid. I'll keep that in mind."

The names of the beginner slopes also make it embarrassing for an adult to be there. The easy slopes have names like, "Potato Patch," or "Fluffy Bunny Hill," or "Mount You Suck." As I got better, meaning I spent more time on my feet than on my face, I was able to go down the more challenging slopes. The difficult slopes are denoted by their extremely disturbing names. Some of these names included, "Ordeal," "Oh No," "Certain Death," and "Is That Part of My Tibia Stabbing Through My Blood Soaked Ski Pants?" I think the easy slopes should have intimidating names as well so that the adults learning how to ski can at least sound cool.

Skier #1: I think I'll ski down Face Laceration and then work my way over to Wet Yourself Hill.
Skier #2: Oh, do they call it that because it's so difficult?
Skier #1: No, it's because it's all four-year-olds down there. They can't get the ski pants off fast enough. You'll be on the black slopes; I'll be on the yellow ones.

I soon became a better skier because I took ski lessons from professionals who are extremely well-trained in hitting on hot ski chicks. However, it was hard to learn anything because the instructors spoke in a ski language which made as much sense to me as "Miss Saigon" performed by sea lions. (See, that didn't make any sense at all.) The instructors would say things like, "On a groomed slope you can carve across the hard-pack much easier than if you're traversing through fresh powder." In an attempt to give some intelligent feedback, I would then say, "My problem is that if

I have eighty percent of the pressure on my outside ski with my edges carved inward while doing an uphill Christie, I still tend to soil myself."

I did have fun on the trip, and as far as I can tell, I survived the entire five days (unless of course Death just hasn't had a chance to collect my earthly soul yet.)

Four Easy Steps to A More Swollen Body

There is an activity that in the past decade has become tremendously important to many Americans. The majority of people find at least a little time for this popular activity because they know their bodies need it to stay healthy and energetic. Some people see it as a hobby; others see it as a way to keep off those extra pounds. I am of course referring to fly fishing. However, since I know nothing about fly fishing, I'm going to talk about exercising.

Everybody's exercising. They're either running, ab rolling, thigh mastering, or health riding. If there is one thing I know about exercising, it's that it's not a ride. You don't have to strap yourself in, you don't have to be a certain height to do it, and there's not much of a chance that the guy in front of you will vomit. So unless exercise acquires these characteristics, which I certainly hope it does, Six Flags doesn't have much to worry about.

Recently I was watching television, and I flipped to "The World's Strongest Man Contest." While I was watching this quality program, it occurred to me that I probably could not roll a car two hundred yards if the need should arise.

Woman: Sir! Sir! My baby is trapped inside this car. Will you please save him by rolling it to those firemen that are two hundred yards in that direction?!
Me: Why don't you just break the win—
Woman: I didn't ask you to talk! Just roll the car!
Me: Yes ma'am.

In order to make sure I would be ready for this all too often occurrence, I started going to the gym to lift weights. I am now a professional at weight-lifting, meaning I once met a guy who had read about it, so I am going to give step-by-step instructions on how to lift weights properly. I guarantee that if you follow my instructions closely, work hard every day, take vitamin supplements regularly, and meditate for a couple hours a week, in three years' time you will be able to look in the mirror and confidently say to yourself, "I want the past three years of my life back."

Step one: What to wear to the gym. Regular shorts and

a tee-shirt will do although there will come a point in your weight-lifting career when you will be forced by the National Foundation of Sweaty Sleeves to cut off the sleeves of all your shirts. This has not happened to me yet, but I've seen it happen to the best of 'em.

Step two: How to attempt to look like you know what you're doing even though everybody else will be able to tell that you have never lifted anything heavier than a large block of cheese. When you first walk in to the weight room, you will most likely think you have accidentally walked in on a tractor pull because many of the guys in there are the size of tractors and consume diesel fuel. However keep in mind that many of them started out just like you, even though the others were most likely manufactured by John Deere. Next, you should find things to lift over your head while making a grunting noise, and then put them back down again. It doesn't really matter what you lift, but weights are the preferred choice. You will probably want to start off with light weights even though many of the other guys in the gym will be benching Range Rovers. After you lift something up and put it down again, you should pose in front of the mirrors for a couple of minutes or until a guy resembling some sort of oak tree backs over you.

Step three: How to talk to other guys in the gym. There is definitely a different language in the gym. Ninety percent of it consists of grunting and the rest is spitting. I believe scratching fits in there somewhere, but I'm not yet fluent.

Step four: When to leave the gym. One good time to leave the workout room is when you've lifted everything in the room over your head at least once and your muscles are as swollen as if you had just gotten in a street brawl with a group of fire ants. Don't worry, this is actually how you want to look. Your goal in weight-lifting is to get to the point when you *always* look like you've had some sort of allergic reaction. Another excellent time to leave the gym is when a man the size of Sweden says to you, "I'm gonna' kick yer' pansy ass."

How to Be A Great Tennis Player: Aim for The Eyes

I started playing tennis at a very young age, and my parents have always been extremely supportive. I fondly remember one warm day in July when I was only six. It was on this day that my father first put a racket in my hand and said, "Son . . . hit your little brother with this if he doesn't stop yelling. If I do it, it's child abuse, but if you do it, it's only sibling rivalry."

As I developed my tennis skills, I became increasingly curious about the finer aspects of the game. I asked questions such as, "How does one hit a topspin serve?," "How should I go about hitting a slice approach shot?," and "Why do women stick the extra tennis balls in their underwear?"

That last question is the one that has never been fully explained to me. I don't know of any other sport where extra balls are shoved down a player's pants. "It's the bottom of the ninth. The pitcher is taking the mound. He is motioning that he needs a ball. Why is Mike Piazza reaching into the crotch of his pants? Wait, he pulled an extra baseball out of his jock strap. How about that!"

I think the players and fans alike would be a lot less accepting if *male* tennis players started storing extra balls in their underwear. I would be the first to object to playing with a tennis ball that had been down Agassi's pants. "Agassi, it really is a privilege to be hitting with you, but can you wait a minute while I run and wash this off? And how about using your pockets from now on?" (Note to reader: I carefully chose not to make a "pulled out the wrong ball" joke, but feel free to make one of your own up.)

With that tennis problem sufficiently discussed, we can now move on to the more important things I've learned about the sport, namely how to get with an attractive tennis player.

Actually, I have almost nothing to say about this topic; I just wanted to get your attention. But I will say this: When trying to win over an attractive tennis enthusiast, don't make jokes about the numerous sexual innuendoes involved in tennis. Anyone who plays tennis on a regular basis has heard them all before and will not be amused. However there is an exception to this rule if the object of your affection is a dirty old man, in which case I have found sexual innuendoes work like a charm.

Tennis is also a very mental sport. Each player must have sound strategy in order to win even the easiest match. I've always had good mental tennis. Here's an example of my thought process during a tennis match. "Why aren't I winning? I should be winning. Forget the match, I'm going to start aiming for his eyes. That'll be fun. . . . Aw, just missed. A little to the left next time. Did I leave the iron on? I don't think so because I don't own an iron. Still, it would be bad if I left it on. I better hurry back to the room and check. Concentrate, you fool. I can win this match. Do I have any underwear on? I sure hope not. I hate playing in underwear; it holds me back. Oh my Gosh, he's coming to net. Whoa, is he aiming for my eyes? That jerk! Did I forget to brush my teeth? I think I did. All that food is sticking to my teeth. It's eating away at them. Ow, it hurts! It's burning! I've got to get it out. Maybe it will help if I stick the ball in my mouth. . . . Okay, okay, I'll take the ball out of my mouth. I wish he would stop yelling at me. If I didn't have to come play this guy, I would have had time to brush. So it's his fault . . . Direct hit! I hit him right in the eye! Uh-oh, he looks hurt. Just walk away casually, and don't look back. He must have poked himself in the eye. It's his word against mine. What if the ball testifies against me? Note to self: pay off ball and don't forget to use the expression, 'You didn't see nothing.'"

As you can see sports drinks have a striking effect on the brain. Well, that's how a regular match goes for me. I hope it is now evident that tennis takes extreme dedication, hard work and a good mental attitude. Tennis is a sophisticated sport for civilized people. So if you're looking for a sport that takes strength, courage and gives you an incredible adrenaline rush, I suggest cow tipping.

7 Statements Not Normally Heard at a Tennis Match

1. You know who's not attractive—that Anna Kournikova girl
2. Advantage Mike Tyson
3. He didn't make it to the wicket, my ass!!
4. The hell with it! Let's just aim for their groins
5. Get your chili dogs while they're hot!
6. Damn, the first round mixed doubles matches are sold out
7. Hey buddy, no touching the girls; only looking. You know the rules

The Three Basic Drives of Men – Sex, Aggression and Sports

Sigmund Freud stated that the human mind revolves around two basic drives: those of aggression and sex. I have recently discovered that he overlooked a third, equally powerful drive which is present in nearly all men—that of the sports drive. (I have some other findings that suggest there is a fourth drive centering around a need for buffalo wings, but more experimentation needs to be done.)

Like any guy, a great deal of my life revolves around sports, a slightly greater amount than revolves around sleeping and eating. But I would probably be viewed as only a moderate sports enthusiast by most men. For example, I don't know who the starting pitcher was on the team that won the 1963 World Series, and in a lot of guy circles, I would be looked down upon for lacking this elementary sports knowledge. I wouldn't be surprised if at least four out of six of my closest friends know the name of that guy and what color underwear he had on during the Series.

Assuming the average human uses about ten percent of his or her brain, at any given moment the average guy is fully devoting at least 9.8 percent to various sports knowledge. This leaves approximately two percent for everything else in his life. In trying to remember so many important sports facts, many men forget other, more trivial, aspects of their lives, such as how many children they are currently fathering. Many people wonder why men often forget to zip up their flies. Well, the reason is that for each time a man remembers to zip his fly, he forgets at least one crucial sports fact.

Guy #1: Hey Frank, your fly's undone.
Guy #2: I know, but it was either forget to zip my fly or forget that the Heisman trophy is named after Coach Johnny Heisman. I chose the former.
Guy #3: Good choice. You gotta' have priorities.

The odd thing about this sports drive is that it is present in athletic men as well as men who could not play fifteen minutes of basketball if it was spread out over thirty years of their life. There are plenty of dedicated sports fans who were bed-ridden for a week following the one and only time they played the highly physical sport of mini-golf, and countless others who view pulling the lever on their Lay-Z-Boy to the "up" position as a day's worth of exercise. These courageous men still find ways to feel involved in the wide world of sports. They yell as many cuss words at their TV during Monday Night Football as the next guy, and they probably write a weekly letter to the coach of their favorite football team advising him on better coaching decisions. "Dear Coach, Please put the team mascot in as the starting linebacker."

There is of course another important sports outlet for athletically impaired men – being a fan for those men who actually can compete. Being a fan is the perfect sport for non-athletic men because it requires absolutely no skill, only extreme devotion and the ability to yell sentences composed entirely of obscenities. Every week thousands of men cheer for sports teams with which they share a bond as deep as marriage. The only difference between it and marriage is that instead of bringing their team flowers, these men wear only their underwear in sub-freezing temperatures and paint their entire bodies with the team's colors. *That's* true love.

Here's another example of the normal guy's idiot sports drive. Let's say he's sitting at a desk with a balled-up piece of paper. There's a trashcan ten feet away, but it's out of his line of sight. He will try to throw the paper ball into the can with a ricochet shot. You may think that the guy did this out of pure laziness, however he will then get up, walk over and check to see if he made the shot. If he did, he will raise his arms and do a brief victory dance, which will include several pelvic thrusts and the ripping off of his shirt. The entire process will take up a great deal more energy and time than just throwing the paper away, yet that will not deprive this heroic man from feeling completely satisfied both as a person and an athlete.

Overall, we sports fans can't understand or control this overwhelming desire to cheer senselessly for our teams; all we can do is hope not to pop a blood vessel in our necks while watching the Playoffs. It is futile to attempt to tame this innate force, and it is actually fortunate that men have found healthy ways to release their need for sports. Otherwise, we would probably wear body paint and Viking helmets at other, less appropriate times, such as job interviews and weddings. (See the cover of this book for an illustration. It will be worth the effort, I promise.)

The Three Basic Drives of Men – Sex, Aggression and More Sports

Due to popular demand, I am presenting you with another sports-related column. (In actuality there was no popular demand unless you count the one faithful reader who requested I set fire to my face.) I wanted to devote a little time to the most popular sports in America—boxing, fishing and lawnmower racing.

I actually saw lawnmower racing on some obscure sports channel the other day. Apparently men get on riding lawnmowers and race around a track. I find it rather pathetic that we've become so desperate for new competitions that we're turning yard work into sports. I want to see the yard work pentathlon.

Referee: Okay contestants, you need to race the lawnmower, plant some tomato seeds, blow the leaves off the deck, fertilize the garden over there and bury the recently deceased family cat in the back yard.

The one thing about lawnmower racing that I do like is if the racer doesn't win the race, he's not a loser, he's a maintenance man. When everybody's asking him why he didn't win, he can just say, "Win what? Were we racing? I was just out there to cut the grass."

You have to wonder how lawnmower racing was invented. I guess some guy was mowing his lawn, realized he's making pretty good time, looked around, noticed his dog couldn't even keep up. He thought to himself, "If there was some kind of lawnmower racing event, I would kick ass." And you know it didn't take long for him to get support for the idea.

Guy: Hey guys, wanna race our lawnmowers?
His friends: Alright!! . . . wait, can we drink beer?
Guy: No, you *have* to drink beer.
His friends: Alright!

And it took him no time to get support from his wife either. "Hold on Ralph, let me get this straight. You and your friends are going to mow our lawn in your spare time? . . . Let the races begin!"

The worst part about the televised lawnmower race I saw was that it was being covered by two announcers. There are actually people who, when asked their profession, respond, "I'm a lawnmower race announcer." How did these people end up doing this? Are they famous, retired lawnmower racers? Are they former lawnmower racers who just couldn't compete in the highly competitive world of professional lawnmower racing?

I do have to give credit to sports announcers, though, for coming up with the weirdest phrase in the English language. I'm referring to the phrase, "letting it all hang out." Think about it: You're in your car, listening to a sports broadcast of what seems like a fairly normal game, and then you hear, "He's goin' for it. He's letting it all hang out." That's when you think to yourself, "What in the hell kind of football game is this?? Good God, that shouldn't be allowed!"

The strangest thing is that we all use this phrase and take

it for granted. We don't even think about the fact that we're talking about someone letting something of theirs just hang out. Who knows exactly what these people are hanging out, but I have a good guess. Also, think about the poor foreigners who come to America and think to themselves, "Wow, that's not legal where I come from, and it only happens when the fans are really drunk." I think this phrase probably originates from the ancient Greeks, but it made sense back then.

Announcer #1: We're getting ready for the second Olympiad, and these marathon runners are really letting it all hang out!
Announcer #2: Yep Jim, no loin cloth for these guys.

On to another sport – boxing. The odd thing about professional boxing is that after a guy gets his ass kicked for a couple of minutes, he stumbles over to his corner, and all he gets in his time of need is a stool. That's all—a stool and some water. These guys are fighting their hearts out; somebody could at least arrange for them to have a chair with a back. If it were up to me, I'd make the fighters feel at home—give them a Lay-Z-Boy and a cold beer in their corner.

Some people consider fishing a sport. Hey, if sitting on a boat, getting a tan and drinking beer is a sport, then sign me up for the intramural team. The thing that amazes me about fishing is that the fish really seem to evade us. It's not easy to catch a fish. I think the reason for this is that we just haven't found a good way to do it yet. In hunting we have guns, crossbows, tranquilizers and even dogs track that scent of the animal. With fish on the other hand, the best idea we've had so far is to put a worm on a hook and wait. We're sending a *worm* down. We're putting the full responsibility of catching the fish on the non-existent shoulders of a *worm*. There has to be a better system. Can't we at least put something with some intelligence on the end of the line, like an eight-year-old? **Fisherman**: Grab the fish, Billy! Grab it! Billy, it's right—Awww, crap!! That's the third kid I've lost this week.

Well, that's all the time I have to talk about weird sports, but maybe some other time we'll get a chance to discuss lumber jack competitions and the no-holds-barred world of competitive jump roping.

Pro-Wrestling –
The Basis of Modern Civilization

With professional wrestling becoming increasingly popular many people are asking the question, "Is pro-wrestling a sport or some other brand of entertainment that resembles a porno movie gone horribly awry?"

Here are the basic qualifications for major sports: Men and/ or women wearing tight clothes, referees making terrible calls, people getting badly injured or killed and screaming idiot fans.

Going by these qualifications alone, one would assume that wrestling is a sport. However, now look at the qualifications for an episode of *The Jerry Springer Show*: Fighting in which chairs are thrown, strange sexual situations, women with chests so big that they have their own gravitational pull and women who look like men and may be men.

Finally, here are the necessary elements of a porn movie: Women with chests so big that they have their own gravitational pull, and people with names like "Mr. Ass" who say things like, "Pimpin' ain't easy."

So essentially pro-wrestling fits into all three of these categories and should be treated accordingly. But if you think about it, has there ever been anything more exciting than a combination of these three genres? Not since the reunion episode of *The Brady Bunch*!

I grew up on pro-wrestling, and to me and my little

brother, Hulk Hogan was a hero. He could do no wrong. We even forgave him for most of his movie roles. My brother and I went to several live wrestling events in which we painted our faces like our favorite wrestlers so that nobody could recognize us as the dorks at the wrestling events.

I was a big fan of the old school wrestlers. King Kong Bundy, Andre The Giant, Big John Stud, Macho Man Randy Savage and The Ultimate Warrior all had lasting influences on me and are most likely responsible for a great deal of emotional trauma inflicted on my innocent mind. It was much like an abusive relationship from which I could not break free.

Me: You are harming my young, fertile mind.
Wrestling: You know you love me. We were made for each other. You're nothing without me!

I'm glad that some of the old wrestlers such as Hulk Hogan and Rick Flair still make appearances now and then, but the truth is at their age they shouldn't be fighting about anything except getting the senior citizen discount at Shoney's. I'm pretty sure Hulk Hogan's skin was removed and replaced with some sort of saran wrap back in the 70's. They should have a World Wrestling Federation for the elderly where old wrestlers can bash each other over the head with their walkers, and the referees are oblivious because at eighty years old their short term memory is that of a coffee table.

My brother and I used to wrestle each other all the time. Our average wrestling match would last until one of us was either pinned or in a coma. As far as I'm concerned, pro-wrestling is not as tough as some people say. If you want to see tough wrestling, watch an eight-year-old attempt to "suplex" his four-year-old brother off a couch onto a hard wood floor. Let me tell you, you can't fake that.

In some ways, you must admit that what the human race has resorted to for entertainment is really sad. We have large men wearing only underwear and body oil get into a ring and pretend to fight while the referee pretends to not notice rule violations. At first this sounds like it's in the same league of bad ideas as John Goodman and Calista Flockhart on a see-saw. I think if aliens came down to earth and saw that pro-wrestling was one of our major forms of entertainment, they would get the hell out of here after doing no more than dumping their waste. But wrestling has succeeded nonetheless, and why shouldn't it?

Without professional wrestling where would thousands of testosterone-filled men go each week in order to see chicks grab each other? Without pro-wrestling where would young politicians go to spring-board themselves into office? Without pro-wrestling where would four-year-olds learn how to tell their friends and teachers to, "suck it?" Our civilization would obviously crumble.

Did You Remember to Align The Gudgeons with The Pintals on The Transom?

If you enjoy wind blowing through your hair, experiencing brief moments of peaceful relaxation, harnessing mother nature's energy and fearing for your life, then sailing is the activity for you!

Don't get me wrong; sailing for long periods of time can be both incredibly fun and highly exhilarating—if you're watching it on television or perhaps listening to someone talk about it.

Seven years ago, my father decided to take this hobby seriously and picked out a brand new catamaran to serve as my family's home away from safety. This was after years of owning a rather pathetic water vehicle that did most of its "sailing" on a trailer in our backyard.

We've had some exciting times on our boat in the past few years. But we've also had many times that would make filling out a tax form seem as exciting as bungee jumping. These beyond-boring periods arise because often there is not enough wind to make the sailboat move at a steady pace. There have been several occasions when my family has been sitting on the boat in the middle of the Chesapeake Bay on a sweltering day cruising along at a brisk 0.0 knots. (For those of you who don't know sailing terminology, 0.0 knots is very slow.)

In these cases, we just sat in our boat watching large, dense rocks do laps around us. Our boat is equipped with two motors, but to a true sailor such as my dad, using the motors is considered cheating in the same way it is considered cheating to eat one of your opponent's rooks during a game of chess. (I don't play chess, but I'm pretty sure that's cheating.)

During these long periods of voluntary boredom, some of us usually go swimming off the boat. We have now learned that before the swimmers can even hit the water, the wind inevitably picks up, often reaching tornado speeds. The swimmers are then left to get stung by a myriad of not-so-friendly jelly fish.

On one trip we brought our dog, Chrissy, with us. We let Chrissy go swimming off the back of the boat and, of course, the wind picked up. With our beloved family dog falling increasingly farther behind the boat, we knew what had to be done. We yelled, "Chrissy, meet us back at the dock!" To which she responded, "Okay! . . . What's a dock?"

It was obvious that we had to take action quickly, but the women on the boat were the only ones smart enough to realize it. So my mom and my pregnant aunt dove into the water to save Chrissy. I finally did something useful by throwing a rope to the three swimmers. My mom, my aunt and the dog were soon securely fastened to the rope by an incredible knot the dog tied, and we pulled them all to safety.

A couple years after my dad first got the sailboat, he decided we needed a smaller, more complicated boat. So he purchased what sailors affectionately call "a dingy." (At this point, I have chosen not to make a distasteful joke about the term "dingy," I'm sorry if I disappointed anyone.)

The dingy was not easy to assemble, and to give you an idea of what we were dealing with, here is one of the real instructions that came with the dingy. "Tie the vang line to the pin on the Becket block, and this will allow the gudgeons to align properly with the pintals on the transom." We spent three hours cursing the fact that the instructions were in German before realizing it was English.

Luckily there were also several vague and meaningless diagrams. Eventually, we put together something remotely resembling a small sail boat and proceeded to never use it again.

There is one more experience on the catamaran which stands out. One summer my family and I were sailing in the Chesapeake Bay, just outside Fort Monroe (not to be confused with Mort's Fun Show). During our trip, a severe storm suddenly hit. The first thing a sailor must do in the event of a storm is sacrifice a small goat to Poseidon. The second thing is to make sure to put the sails down.

My dad attempted to pull in the jib (the jib being the smaller, much more evil sail), but since we were in the middle of fifty mile-per-hour winds, the rope simply cut through his hand like a Ginsu knife through an old shoe.

After my dad's hand was lacerated, we all took shelter inside the boat while it drifted aimlessly in the turbulent waters. My younger brother and I eased the tension by singing the theme song to *Gilligan's Island*.

Soon the storm subsided, and we continued on our way to Fort Monroe in order to get my dad some medical attention. A Coast Guard boat actually came up next to us on our way in, but my dad, not wanting to be a pansy about his third-degree rope burns, yelled that we were doing fine. The Coast Guard probably wondered about the bloody dish towel wrapped around his hand.

When we finally arrived at the dock, we noticed a broad assortment of emergency personnel waiting for my dad, including two fire trucks, three police cars, two military police and one ice cream truck.

My dad was quite embarrassed that all the emergency personnel were there to treat his hand, so he quickly asked me to shove an oar through my spleen to give the good people something to do.

Ultimately, my dad's hand fully healed, and my family and I have learned our lesson: We've returned to doing all our sailing on a trailer in the backyard.

Extreme Bowling Found
To Be Extremely Nauseating

One night last week some friends and I were sitting around doing absolutely nothing—or maybe something a little more boring than that—when I decided I wanted to participate in an activity that involved wearing old shoes, hurling fourteen-pound balls and drinking beer. Could such a wondrous sport actually exist? Yes, but it's illegal in three states. So we settled for bowling.

When we entered the bowling alley, we were overwhelmed by flashing strobe lights, pumping music and the actual smell of obesity. This was not what I expected in a bowling alley (except for the obesity thing). Apparently there is one night a week when the bowling alley combines bowling with bad music and disco lighting. Many bowling alleys have termed this activity "extreme bowling." I don't know exactly why this is necessary or fun or necessarily fun. It might be possible that "fun" is actually measured by the size of the headache one gets afterwards, in which case I had a hell of a time.

I don't even think "extreme bowling" deserves its name. The term "extreme bowling" should be reserved for bowling on icebergs in Antarctica or bowling in the personal territory of an adult mountain lion. That's extreme bowling. What these bowling alleys have in fact set up is more along the lines of "obnoxious bowling" or "nauseating bowling." Just because they turn off the lights and play Britney Spears does not make the bowling "extreme" in any way. If you think about it in terms of other sports, it doesn't work either. If you turn off the lights and play Britney Spears at a football game, it doesn't become extreme – you just get your ass kicked.

My friends and I eventually came to terms with the fact that we were going to be bowling in a disco club atmosphere and proceeded to pay a lot of money to wear used shoes. Can anything really be called a "sport" if it doesn't include wearing shoes that have held the sweat and fungus of hundreds of people you've never met and probably would not want to get anywhere near? I think not.

The bowling shoes I was given should have been put in either a museum or a lab for culturing bacteria. I think there should be a professional bowling shoe smeller guy, and if he has a cardiac arrest when he smells a pair of shoes, the shoes should be retired from bowling for good. They should be put in a little bowling shoe retirement home where all the nasty shoes could hang out together instead of adding to the already oppressive foulness of most bowling alleys. The sports community retires jerseys of professional sports players all the time, and let me tell you, it's not because that particular player was really good. It's because he or she left such a funk in the jersey that it needed to be put in a museum somewhere just to air out.

If you think about it, bowling shoes are the prostitutes of the shoe community. They're with a different man or woman every night, you have to pay for them and they don't care what you look like. I don't know about you, but I don't really enjoy having to wear shoe whores just to go bowling. Who knows what kind of diseases they have? Besides, I don't think my pair really cared about me anyway. They just wanted the money.

My friends and I finally went to our lanes and started bowling. I originally learned how to bowl at a camp that offered bowling as one of the daily activities. Needless to say, most of the kids' time there was spent lofting bowling balls at each other. So I don't exactly have a professional bowling background.

There are many different bowling techniques. One is to put spin on the ball while another is to push the ball lightly down the middle of the lane. My personal strategy is to launch the ball as far as humanly possible and hope to decapitate or maim many of the pins. I have been using this strategy for several years now, and it has done pretty well for me. I think I've had a great amount of anger towards bowling pins in general ever since one was hired to kill my brother three years ago. My bowling technique is often not successful in knocking down all the pins, however several of them do wet themselves. I believe the key to any sport is intimidation, and every time it's my turn I can tell the front pin is scared out of his mind.

That night we paid for the "all-you-can-bowl" offer just in case we felt the need to set up tents and start our families right there in the bowling alley. (Some of the people next to us had done this.) In our first game I bowled rather poorly, knocking down more fellow bowlers than pins. In our second game I finally figured out that I needed to loft the ball a little further and attempt to hit the pins on the fly. This strategy worked much better. Unfortunately, the high-tech scoring computer at our lane was acting as drunk as some of our fellow bowlers. It began completely screwing up the scoring. I'm very sympathetic, though, because I would have a better chance of doing all of Microsoft's taxes correctly in Japanese than I would of scoring a game of bowling correctly. As far as I can tell, the equation for scoring a game of bowling is as follows:

number of pins knocked down – twice bowler's weight x % of funk in your shoes + (number of turkeys you've eaten) / how many beers you've had

Later in the game I did actually get a "goose" or a "turkey" or whatever it's called, but in spite of my heated argument with the manager, they wouldn't give me an actual turkey. Even with this setback I found bowling to be an exhilarating sport. I do, however, get the same exhilaration from dropping watermelons out a fourth story window, and I can do that without wearing a nasty pair of shoes.

7 Ways to Liven-up Bowling

1. Replace balls with live armadillos
2. Anybody who does a dumb victory dance after bowling a strike receives a minor shock
3. Less bowling shoes; more roller skates
4. If you bowl a gutter ball, ball is shot back at you at forty miles per hour
5. You must keep score with an abacus
6. Hit The Guy With The Goofy Shirt Night
7. Different "gooey surprise" in finger holes of every ball

5
Technology

Warning: Do Not Use Your Cordless Phone near This Humor Column

I would like to bring to your attention an extremely grave situation that in the near future could affect every last one of us. However, I couldn't find such an issue, so I'm going to talk about the time I went to buy a new cordless phone. (I know, it's random. But whatcha' gonna' do?) Reading my account of striving for cordless bliss may spawn fond memories of your own cordless phone, in which case, you're clinically insane.

This past summer I began having trouble with the telephone in my room. The first problem was the malfunction of the number two. I solved this by only calling people without any two's in their phone numbers. However, the sickness spread like a cancer, and soon the four and five buttons succumbed to the illness. The Chemotherapy was unsuccessful, so I broke down and went to buy a new phone.

I decided to purchase a cordless phone so that I could talk on it while up to three feet away from the base. (Can you feel the excitement?) The first salesperson I talked to quickly demonstrated his ability to sound extremely informative while still basically saying, "I don't know." I then found another salesperson who was having some sort of seizure. The third employee I spoke to finally helped me make my purchase.

Once I got home, I started reading the instructions for my phone. It was reassuring to see that the instructions for screwing in the antenna came complete with a diagram of which way is clockwise. If you don't know which way clockwise is, should you really be allowed to operate a telephone?

Next I had to select a location for my phone. To my surprise, (I'm not making this up) the instructions suggested that the phone be placed away from electrical machinery (such as a cappuccino machine), electrical appliances (such as a cappuccino machine), metal walls or filing cabinets, wireless intercoms, Toyota Camrys, and professional soccer teams (I made those last two up). Then it said the phone should not be near (I swear this is true) other cordless phones. I guess otherwise territorial disputes would break out.

The instructions then read, "Note: You must not connect your phone to any coin-operated systems." This particularly upset me because I was planning on hooking my phone up to a vending machine in hopes that I would be able to communicate with the Ho-Ho's. The instructions also told me to try several different locations and "see which provides the best performance." I hate to break it to the geniuses who wrote the instruction booklet, but I'm going to put my phone where I'm going to be making phone calls. I just can't see doing otherwise.

"Hey Lee, can I use your phone?"

"Yeah, sure, it's downstairs under the fold-out sofa. Excellent reception."

Another note in the instructions said that if my phone line was not a modular jack, the wiring needed to be updated. It said I could update the wiring myself. Two paragraphs previous the directions were showing me which way is clockwise, and now they expected me to update my phone wiring to a modular jack?

Well, knowing a little something about electronics, I carefully took a fork and JABBED IT INTO THE PHONE JACK! After several volts passed through my body, I realized that the phone jack was actually the thermostat. Later I also found out that I already had a modular outlet.

Next I read the topic about setting the volume. It said, "adjust the *Volume* to control the volume of the sound you hear through the handset." This surprised me because up until that point I thought that the *Volume* controlled the volume of everybody standing around me.

There was also a section called "Testing Stored Emergency Numbers." The instructions told me that when testing a stored emergency number I should, "remain on the line to explain the reason for [my] call." It was lucky they told me that because I was just going to call 911 and shout, "Man with gun! Dear God!" and hang up. I didn't know that was frowned upon.

Finally, some warnings about the phone were presented. It said, "Use and store the phone only in normal temperature environments." I realized that meant I had to stop using the phone while I was in my freezer. It also meant that I had to leave my phone at home whenever I travel to the oven-like planet of Venus.

Despite the ingenious instructions, my phone works perfectly. Whenever I'm home, I bask in my cordless bliss. I just lay there talking on the phone and laughing at the base, whose restraints I have cast aside. However, I have to stay under my desk while I'm laughing at the base because that's the only place I get clear reception.

Computers Take over Toys, The World

I am worried about the growing rate of incredible technological advancements such as the internet, motorized tie racks and Pepsi One. Machines are slowly taking over the home and workplace. Not only are jobs becoming obsolete, but so are humans. I'm not even writing this; I started to write it, and then my laptop said I wasn't doing a good job and took over.

Actually there is a little man in my word processor who I believe is taking over my life. (I know that last sentence sounded like I need a team of psychiatrists working on me, but just keep reading.) For anybody who has Windows, the help menu in Microsoft Word sends out a little animated paperclip man with eyes, a big smile and a bad attitude. Usually you have to request this paperclip man to come out, but sometimes he will just invite himself out to annoy you.

For example, if I begin typing a letter, he will pop up and say, "It looks like you're typing a letter, would you like some help?" Then I angrily type into the question box, "Your mother is a twisty tie." With a huge smile he responds to this (I'm not making this up) by asking me if I would like help "breaking a connection to a linked object." Finally, I click on "close" to make him leave, and right before he disappears, he gives me a goodbye wink as if we're buddy-buddy. In order to truly understand how this sociopathic paperclip found his way into personal computers, a brief history is useful.

A long time ago, before the Bible began and just after a young Dick Clarke got into show business, the first computer was developed. It was built by a group of middle-aged men who had never been with a woman and thought that Captain Kirk was their best friend. The computer they so diligently constructed was about the size of the Loch Ness monster and could, when asked the square root of four, display a naked image of Bill Gates. Although this initial computer was not practical for home use, it was the start of the computer revolution.

A couple of years later the men most of us lovingly refer to as "computer nerds" made the next step in personal computers by developing the first chat room. The chat room made it possible for a nerd in one room to convince a nerd in another room that he was an eighteen-year-old Playboy bunny wearing only a thong. The most important step for personal computers was taken a couple years later when a word processing system was developed that included an annoying animated paperclip. However, this was only the beginning of the confusing features of personal computers.

To better understand computers many of us buy the self-help books made "For Dummies." These books are basically saying, "People who need this book are stupid," and yet the books are still extremely popular. There are also self-help books "For Idiots." The people who buy the "Idiots" version are basically confessing that the "Dummies" series was just way over their heads. I'm waiting for the books like, "Word Processing For People Who Know Less About Computers Than Their Hamsters," or "The Internet For People Whose IQ's Are That Of Cottage Cheese."

But computers are not the only super confusing things on the market. Even toys are beginning to go over our heads. In the past few years Furbies and mechanical dogs have been very popular, and they can actually tell the child how to play with them. Unfortunately I've never gotten the opportunity to be ordered around by a Furby, but I hear they can tell a child such things as, "Boring," "I'm hungry," or "Bring me your father's gun, and don't ask questions."

You do have to wonder how long it will be until these robotic beings get tired of being chased around the kitchen floor by a cat and decide to do something truly sinister, like run for Congress.

I was recently walking through a drug store when one of the stuffed animals on the shelf blurted out to me, "I love you. Give me a hug!" I was shocked to hear this. I barely knew the stuffed penguin, and I had no idea she felt that way.

All I'm trying to say is that the computerized world can be scary, and you should keep a close eye on your laptop because, if you give it the chance, it will process you and everyone you care about. As long as we keep technology in check, it can definitely be a good thing. For example, technology helped me find true love. The stuffed penguin and I have plans to marry even though our children may have wings and require two AA batteries.

7 Things Not Commonly Found in A Desk

1. Happiness
2. Dick Clarke
3. Metaphysical transcendence
4. Lake Erie
5. Two of the Three Stooges
6. Shrimp fried rice
7. A good time

6

Pets

Tell The Chef This Dog Food Is Superb

As a young adult, there are certain things I think we all miss while we're away from our families. Not being able to see your parents, your siblings and old friends for months or years at a time isn't that bad. But I miss my dog.

I think owning pets is wonderful because they can be your best friends and keep you company at all times—except the African swooping bird, which will fly straight into your head if you attempt to get near it or even have brief thoughts of fondness towards it.

I do have an opinion as to what types of animals make the best and worst pets, but I'll keep those feelings to myself because they might offend other pet owners.

All iguanas should be killed. Iguanas are bitter little animals with sharp claws and a desire to maim those they care about most. In high school, a friend of mine once asked me to baby-sit his iguana while he was away. Unfortunately, I thought he said "Wanda," his gorgeous twenty-five-year-old sister. I didn't understand why she needed baby-sitting at that age, but I thought it was a good idea nonetheless. Then my friend told me she was sick and would need a shot of medicine in her upper thigh twice a day. Also, she was having trouble with bladder control. Finally, he told me that during the vast majority of the day she enjoys finding something warm to rub up against. At this point, I was weighing the pros and cons. She was an attractive twenty-five-year-old woman who liked to cuddle. On the other hand, she had bladder problems. I boldly decided I would take the bad with the good.

The next day, I found out my friend had actually said "iguana," not "Wanda." Unfortunately I had already agreed to undertake the task and soon discovered the iguana was not all too happy to have a complete stranger stabbing her in the upper thigh with a needle. I survived the week of pet-sitting, but the iguana and I did not become close friends. I'm just glad she was high on medication when I was looking after her because when she's healthy, she can knock a grown man's face off using only her tail.

But don't think I hate all pets. My family has owned a wonderful black lab for the past nine years named Chrissy (or Charlotte, or something with a "ch" at the beginning). Chrissy is a wonderful dog because she's loyal and smart and I can blame her whenever I throw up on the carpet. The point being that pets serve many purposes.

For example, throughout high school it was Chrissy's job to wake me up in the morning. Every morning she came to my room, jumped on my bed and clawed at my trachea until I woke up. Of course, occasionally she failed at her assignment. Sometimes she just sat in my room calmly until I eventually woke up an hour late for school.

When this happened, I yelled at Chrissy's supervisor, or "Mom," as I called her. My mother always said, "She didn't wake you up? That's odd."

The truth is, Chrissy's a smart dog, and I would not trade her for anything in the entire world – except perhaps some sort achievements in her lifetime that prove her a worthy pet. Here's a list of her accomplishments.

1. Scratching herself
2. Being able to open the screen door with her forehead
3. Eating an entire bag of flour when nobody was home
4. Chewing up the blue Frisbee

Despite all the fun pets provide, they are a big responsibility – in fact a bigger responsibility than most household appliances. One of the things that makes taking care of animals so difficult is buying their food.

When I went to look for dog and cat food recently, I found it difficult to chose a specific type. A few of the types offered were "casserole dinner," "shrimp and fish feast," and "fresh water trout in sauce." There's something wrong when my cat is eating fresh water trout and I'm munching on stale Pop-Tarts. Who do you think wears the pants in that relationship? (Oddly enough, my cat does insist on wearing my pants.)

There was also a type called "Savory Entrée." You have to wonder, how do the manufacturers know this dog food is savory? They must taste it – there's no other way. And then you have to ask yourself, "Do I really want to buy dog food from human beings who eat dog food?" That's a question that will keep you up at night.

And does a dog really care if the meat is savory? Last I checked, my dog gets extremely excited when I let her lick mustard off the bottom of my shoe. I don't think she's going to be picky about the savory grilled sirloin. We could package dog food called "mustard off the bottom of a shoe," and the dogs would love it just the same.

Then there was "Master's Choice" dog food. Who is this master who's picking types of dog food? That's sort of like being the master Port-O-Potty cleaner – You may be the master, but you're still hating life.

There was also dog food which was a "chef's blend." If you're an aspiring chef and you find yourself cooking up canned dog food for a living, it's officially time to let go of the dream. It just isn't working out.

There was even a type of treats called "charbroiled steaks" with the little black grill lines on them. The manufacturers really expect us to believe there is a guy slaving over a grill, flipping doggy treats? "Oh yeah, these are cookin' real nice. Hey Honey, could you find out if Sammy the Border collie wanted medium or well-done?"

I finally chose some canned dog food called "Your Dog Won't Know The Difference." Only the best for my pet.

Elvis Fathered My Hamsters

When I was a mere fifth-grader growing up in the jungles of South America, (well actually I was told it was South America, but really my parents had locked me in the back yard for several years) my family stumbled upon an extraordinary scientific discovery equal in magnitude to the formula for beef jerky. Since then I have come to the realization that our findings must be relayed to the masses before anyone else gets hurt or, worse yet, pregnant.

It all began when my older brother, Marshall, was in high school. For a class experiment he decided to see if different types of music affect the number of times a hamster will run around a wheel. (Even at that young age he was contemplating the true mysteries of the universe.)

The first step in the experiment was to go out and buy a hamster, or at least something with a lot of fur that could be passed off as a hamster. It didn't take us long to decide on one at the pet store. However, it did take the employee awhile to tell us whether our hamster was male or female, but the man eventually found out the hamster was male because its favorite television show was *Bay Watch*.

We weren't going to have any sissy hamsters in our house, so we named the poor, little creature Bob. Bob took his position in his cage downstairs and what I loosely refer to as "science" was ready to begin. Marshall set the stereo so that it would play an Elvis CD all night long. The next morning we recorded the number of times Bob had run around the wheel.

As the days went by, Marshall played a different type of music for Bob each night. Each type of music had a different effect on Bob.

Elvis – Bob's sideburns got bigger
Rap – Bob began to refer to his cage as his "crib"

Easy Listening – Bob did not run around the wheel, but instead banged his head against the cage repeatedly
The Beatles – Bob thought he was bigger than Jesus
Alternative – Bob refused to bathe for long periods of time
Elvis (a second time) – Bob had babies

Actually, it's absolutely, completely, I-wish-I-was-lying-but-I'm-not true that after we played Elvis for the second time, Bob gave birth to approximately eight little pink objects, which, following further examination, were revealed to be baby hamsters. At first this created a great confusion within the scientific community consisting of my family and our dog. We soon realized that what we had discovered was tremendous: An exorbitant amount of Elvis can cause pregnancy in any species in either gender. Is there anything "The King" can't do?

My family agreed then and there to forget about our hopes of winning a Nobel prize and never tell the general public about the horrors that had taken place in our basement. We agreed to return Bob and his pink objects to the pet store and if we ever heard Elvis music, to run away in fear of spontaneously giving birth to many hamsters.

If our society doesn't learn to avoid Elvis music soon, people will be having hamster-children all over the place. Then the problem is that mothers (male or female) will have trouble explaining to their hamster-children who the father is.

Child: Mom, who's my daddy?
Mother: Um, well Billy, do you know who Elvis is?
Child: Yeah, we saw him singing for nickels on a street corner.
Mother: Okay, have you heard the song, "Jailhouse Rock?"
Child: No.
Mother: Well, that's your father. I played that song about

20,000 times while I was high in college, and then I had you.
Child: Oh. Why am I nocturnal?
Mother: You ask too many questions. Get back in your cage.

Now that the truth is out, the responsibility lies in the hands of the public. Stay away from Elvis music and protect your pets from it too. Also don't force your pets to listen to country music. It doesn't cause pregnancy, but it is a form of animal abuse.

7 Uses for Live Hamsters

1. Dust those hard to reach spaces
2. Put in outgoing mail bin to lighten office atmosphere
3. Liven-up a simple game of catch
4. Put in with child's pile of stuffed animals, and watch funny reaction (May also cause schizophrenia)
5. Send in to repair jammed computer disk drive
6. Someone to bounce ideas off of
7. Fun centerpiece at formal dinners

7

Holidays & Vacations

Halloween Past, Present and Frat Party

Halloween has a complex history. If I was an historian, I might inform you that the first Halloween occurred completely by accident in the 1600's in Sicily when a drunken mule ran headlong into the town dwarf, but I would of course be insane. The truth is that I don't know the history of Halloween.

I do know that Halloween is one day a year when people of all ages can have a good time. Children walk through their neighborhoods collecting candy, adults enjoy the looks on the children's faces as candy is dished out and college kids steal the candy from the defenseless children. I'm kidding of course; it's ridiculous to think that the adults actually enjoy giving out candy.

When we were kids, the best part of Halloween was collecting candy. Of course there were some people that were a little stingy with the candy. They'd give you "Fun Size." Not so fun, was it? The candy companies want kids to believe that the "Fun Size" candies have been designed for optimal fun, that fun is guaranteed. I think those candies should be called "Crap Size." Because when you were eight, if you opened your

Halloween bag and saw Fun Size candy looking up at you, you didn't yell, "Oh, fun!" You said, "Oh crap!"

If you have a brother or sister, you are probably familiar with the candy bargaining which followed trick-or-treating. The second we got home, my brother and I would become professional candy-traders. "I'll give you four Snickers and a Smarties for two of your Reeses Cups and half a pack of Spree. Do you like caramel? No? How about the crispidy crunchiness of a Kit Kat bar? What do you mean you don't like Kit Kats?! They're crispidy. They're crunchidy. They're wafers smothered in milk chocolate! Alright, fine. I'll give you my entire Fun Size population for your candy apple. You run a hard bargain, little man."

I find the most annoying part of Halloween is picking a costume. (The second most annoying thing is finding out too late that your costume doesn't have a fly.) Picking a costume is tough because it's your one chance each year to let loose, forget all your inhibitions and simply say, "I want to be a European crack-whore, and I don't care what anyone thinks about it!" However, don't say it too loud or you'll get arrested, at least in every state other than Nebraska.

I always used to dress up as the same thing every year. I was some kind of man with a third eye ball on his forehead and needles through his face. For this costume my brother and I began by applying pounds of "fake skin" to our faces. For those of you who have never seen this stuff, "fake skin" seems to be a mixture of Vaseline and hair, and when carefully applied to our faces, made it look like we had fallen asleep in a vat of Vaseline and hair. We then stuck needles, paper clips and safety pins through this fake skin in order to take on the appearance of ghastly men who had either been in a horrible sewing accident or were trying to run an office supply store out of their faces.

Halloween gets weird in college. For example, one year my roommate decided on a costume that gave him an air of both dignity and manliness – a full-body Winnie the Pooh outfit. I have absolutely nothing against Pooh or those who choose to dress like him. In fact, I support Pooh in all his exploits, whether it be finding honey or changing his name to something more respectable, like Rob. However, I must admit that during the Halloween party, there was something unsettling about watching Winnie the Pooh smoke Marlboros and throw down Budweisers. After hearing many Pooh stories and even watching him on TV, I was almost positive that Pooh was more of a Miller Lite man.

You just don't have the same opinion of your childhood heroes after watching them get trashed at a party. "Well, He-Man is in the corner hitting on Little Orphan Annie. I think that's Mr. Rogers dancing to 'Back That Ass Up,' with Papa Smurf oddly enough. And it looks like Elmo just passed out in that trash can."

Long live Halloween.

The Little Van That Couldn't

Several years ago my family and I went on a vacation to Martinique, a quaint little island with lovely beaches and roads paved mostly out of bull dung. The national pastime there is laughing at tourists, and the national bird can peck a grown man's eyes out in seconds. Martinique is actually a province of France, therefore when I say the national past time is making fun of tourists, that is France's pastime as well.

To have fun on the island, we decided to rent a car, drive up some mountain roads and hike further up a dormant volcano. This trip didn't seem that tough, as long as we had the G.I. Joe special forces at our disposal.

On the morning of the journey we were all ready to go. By "ready" I mean we had about half our weight in insect repellent lathered on our skin. The insects didn't stay away from us; they just became fossilized in a flood of repellent. I think that's actually the truth about those mosquitoes found fossilized in amber from the dinosaur age. That's no amber; it's actually a chunk of bug repellent that fell off a primitive tourist who was trying to repel mosquitoes the size of his face.

Primitive kid: Dad, I want to see the triceratops *up close*!!
Primitive tourist dad: Shut up and put on more bug repel-lent.

Back to the incoherent story at hand. My family and I rented a crappy little European car. Once in the car, we tried to find our way up the mountain using only a map that resembled a diagram of McDonalds' play land. Soon we turned off of the "main road" and onto what the map called a "secondary road." Apparently this meant that the road was secondary in quality to, say, a rundown mountain bike trail. Keep in mind that we were in a small French mini-van which must have been powered by a single nine-volt battery. For some reason we got stuck half way up one of the inclines (take note of the heavy sarcasm).

All of us got out of the van except my dad, who floored it and got the van up that particular hill. The rest of us began hiking up the road after the car. While hiking, I noticed something on the side of the road. I decided to inform the others without frightening them. So I calmly pointed and yelled, "BUUUULLLLL!!!" My family and I bolted up the road with our legs moving in a circular motion like the Road Runner. We then looked back and realized that the bull I had seen was actually chained to the side of the road. This, however, did not stop me from running until I was well into my thirties.

Meanwhile my father realized that our rented matchbox car was not going to make the journey, at least not as long as the trip entailed going uphill. My father then attempted to turn the van around. While he was doing this, a little European car drove up, and the man inside said something urgent in French. For the first time that day I successfully communicated myself in French by saying, "I can't speak French." Since we didn't speak the same language, the man used several hand gestures and a cartoon he quickly sketched to express to me that my dad was about to back off a cliff.

After deciding against that particular turn-around spot, it seemed the only clear place to turn around was by the bull. By "clear" I mean blocked off by a massive animal with horns. Luckily, the bull merely watched and laughed hysterically at our situation. Once my dad had turned the van around, he roared down the incline at the van's full speed (equal to the top speed of a wild cheetah with only one leg). We watched as the "Little European Van That Could Not" flew up the incline and out of our sight. My dad used the momentum to take him straight on to Indonesia. The rest of us were left hiking after him.

Eventually we got in the van and retreated away from the volcano. We actually saw an excessive amount of nature that day, much of it was of the stinging variety. I learned that to make such a journey, one should obtain a guide, a gondola and the G.I. Joe special forces including Snake Eyes and Sergeant Slaughter.

Nothing Says USA like Gravy

Thanksgiving is quite frankly the best holiday of the year for one simple reason: you can consume enough gravy to fill an Olympic-size swimming pool three times over and no one will look at you funny. Thanksgiving is wonderful because it is a day of being thankful for what we have, followed a month later by a holiday in which we're thankful for everything people have bought us.

Thanksgiving was first celebrated by Pilgrims arriving in the new world. They wanted to celebrate the fact that they were still alive after eating nothing but rats and undercooked boot leather during an extremely long boat trip. The adults in the group were also celebrating the end of a five month period during which their children said nothing but, "Are we there yet?"

The Pilgrims weren't sure how they wanted to celebrate the new holiday, so they looked to the Bible and their friends, the Native Americans, for help. The Native Americans suggested dining on buffalo tongues. The Pilgrims took the advice but eventually substituted "buffalo tongues" with "yams." They then found a passage in the Bible that read, "The Lord will cometh with large quantities of bright red, soul-devouring fire." The Pilgrims simply replaced "soul-devouring fire" with "cranberry sauce," and they had themselves a holiday.

Thanksgiving is interesting because it seems every family has their own traditions for this special occasion. For example, some families have ham instead of turkey while others cover their first born male in guacamole.

My family actually has two unusual traditions. One is taking a hike on Thanksgiving morning, and the other is Russians (I'll explain in a moment). Our hike is usually over a bridge to a small island in the James River. We do this in hopes that one of our guests will break his or her ankle, and we won't have to feed as many people. The hike is great fun and often thins out the ranks considerably. One has to qualify to eat Thanksgiving dinner with my family; we don't just give away spots at our table.

Your chances of dining with us will be greatly enhanced, however, if you're Russian. For several years my mom has been active in helping Jewish Russian immigrants set up a new life here in the land of opportunity and coffee shops. We usually have between two and eighty Russians over to our house in order to show them a good Thanksgiving. There is obviously no Thanksgiving in Russia because there is no American football, a crucial ingredient of the holiday.

The conversations at our Thanksgiving table are quite intriguing. Here's a brief sample.

Boris: What is Pilgrim?
Me: Uh, people that looked a little like the Amish.
Boris: What is Amish?
Me: Uh, you know. They have the wagons, and . . .
Boris: Oh, like donkeys?
Me: Not exactly. They look like Abraham Lincoln. Do you know who he is?
Boris: Yes. He stole my radio last month.

Me: No, that's not—
Boris: Yes he did! He's jerk. Well, then I don't like Pilgrims.
Me: Me neither.
Boris: What is stock market?

I am not trying to imply that the Russians at our Thanksgivings aren't very smart—most of them know more about America and our system of government than I do. I am simply saying that there is definitely a bit of a language barrier.

Following the meal, my family and I usually spend about three hours trying to teach the Russians the rules to American football.

Me: They try to get the ball to the other end of the field.
Alexander: Can they use automobile?
Me: No, but they can use men that weigh as much as automobiles. If they get the ball to the other end, they get six points, but they can get another point if they kick the ball through the yellow poles or they can get two more points if they get the ball in the end zone a second time.
Alexander: So this makes possible to get 30,000 points in one chance?
Me: I've never really thought of it that way.
Alexander: Is vodka involved?
Me: Only after they've won the game. Anyway, right now we need to cheer for our team.
Alexander: Rip out spines of other team and show bleeding bodies to wife and children! Is this good cheer?
Me: Excellent.
Alexander: This whole experience is so . . . What is word?
Me: Constipating?
Alexander: Yes. This is constipating. All of America is constipating.
Me: I couldn't agree more.

Thanksgiving is a crucial holiday because after all, what would America be if there wasn't at least one day a year that included gorging ourselves until pure fat oozed out our ears, watching grown men knock the life out of each other and sleeping for about twelve hours? Actually, I think I do that every Sunday.

Thank You! It's Just What I Never Wanted

I hope everybody had a good holiday season. (And I hope you just enjoyed generic opening sentence number 143.) Un-fortunately, with the holidays comes shopping. In my opinion shopping has all the redeeming qualities of strep throat. I, like the majority of guys, don't enjoy shopping. My problem is I'm not good at shopping for other people. During most holidays I find myself saying, "You mean you didn't want a terminally ill spider monkey?"

Gift certificates are my savior though. They stop me from buying something incredibly stupid, like two pounds of veal for my vegetarian cousin. However, giving someone a gift certificate is basically saying, "I didn't know what the hell to get you. I hate shopping in general, so you go do it yourself. Go pick something out; you can pretend I got it for you, but just leave me out of the entire process."

The only problem with gift certificates is that store employees never know what to do with them. When you try to redeem one, the employee always acts like it's the first time he's ever seen one. After a few futile attempts at registering it, he usually starts asking the other cashiers. "Guys, what do I do with this? Can he pay with this? Do we really give these things out? It's just a piece of paper. I don't think he can do that."

Suddenly all the employees are running around like an agitated ant farm training for a marathon. The workers try to comfort you while you're waiting there. "We're working on the situation, sir. All we've got here is a cash register. It registers cash. You gave us some sort of certificate instead." Finally a head manager comes out who apparently dealt with a similar situation during the Reagan administration. He always has a special key around his neck and knows the secret access codes. For some reason redeeming a gift certificate is like firing nuclear missiles. "Three, two, one. (Key is turned.) We have gift certificate!"

Cash is a good present too. Whenever someone gives you money, they always say, "I want you to use it to buy yourself something nice." Yet most of the time we never do that. We use the money to pay for something practical, like gas or groceries. But wouldn't it be weird if the person took that extra step and gave you gasoline for your birthday? "Here you go. I figured if I gave you money, you'd just use it for gas anyway, so here's five gallons. It's not much, but you can use it as fuel for your car or maybe to set fire to someone you dislike." Or what if they got you some practical household items? "Happy birthday. I just picked up a pack of raw mushrooms, a toilet bowl brush and some margarine. They're yours to keep."

It bothers me that every advertisement over the holidays acts like their product is a perfect gift. It doesn't matter what it is. "Having trouble finding a gift for the guy that has everything? Tired of shopping? Well, here's the answer! Goldbond Medicated Powder! It's perfect for any man, as well as some unusual women! Also comes in cream form!"

I actually heard a commercial that said a lottery ticket is a great gift for the holidays. Who gives someone a lotto ticket for Christmas? I'm sorry, but that's a crappy gift. "Here you go, buddy. Your chances of winning aren't too good. In fact, you've got a better chance of being attacked in your living room by a hippopotamus wearing a top hat. But if you do win, it will be like I gave you two million dollars! Wouldn't that be one hell of a Christmas gift?!" Giving someone a lotto ticket as a gift is like giving them a box that *could* have a big screen TV in it but most likely is full of scrap metal.

Believe it or not, I don't enjoy opening presents either. I can't stand having to act excited when someone gives me a gift. "Oh my God! This is wonderful! How could you have known?! . . . Can I have the receipt?"

The worst thing you can do after giving someone a gift is following up on it. If they seem remotely happy, never ask them about it again. You're only setting yourself up to hear the worst lying since the O.J. trial.

You: I haven't seen you wearing that shirt I gave you.
Your friend: Well, it was the craziest thing. I took it with me to,

uh, Jamaica, and while I was there, um, it was stolen. They ran by me and grabbed it!

You: While you were wearing it?

Your friend: It was the damnedest thing.

You: And they were able to pull it over your head and off your body as they ran by?

Your friend: I was impressed as well. They were obviously professionals.

I hope I've given you some useful tips on how to do your shopping. If you have anymore questions, I'll be at the mall buying my brother a toilet bowl brush for his birthday.

German Sausage Is Coming Back Up: A Guide to Amusement Parks

Like the majority of jaded Americans looking to waste half their life savings in a single summer outing, I went to an amusement park this past August. At this point I would like to put to rest anybody's fear that I might be tempted to make sexual innuendoes concerning the name of the amusement park I went to – Busch Gardens. I will actively avoid such obscene references, and any that are found are merely the result of readers' sick minds.

I began the day by getting quite excited about entering Busch Gardens. Once inside I was eager but also a bit overwhelmed. I was, however, impressed by my stamina inside Busch Gardens and pleased at how well I knew my way around even though it was my first time. Afterwards I was quite exhausted, yet couldn't wait for my next escapade inside those incredible gardens.

After parking my car I had to walk approximately thirty-four miles to the park entrance. The park is as spaced out as possible in order to cause dehydration and force tourists to buy twenty-two gallons of lemonade at three dollars a cup.

Once at the gate, I had to purchase a ticket which goes up in price four dollars every five minutes. In general, if you were at the park last summer and the tickets cost twenty-four dollars each, then when you return this summer, each ticket will cost 25,000 dollars.

The first thing I noticed inside Busch Gardens was that I could think of nothing more painful than being an employee there. As an employee you would, of course, deal with stupid, tired and sometimes pissed-off customers who would likely walk up to you and, despite the fact you are standing in front of a sign that lists every beverage available, would ask which drinks you have to offer. They would then request the only drink you did not list.

Employee: We have Pepsi, Diet Pepsi, Mountain Dew, Dr. Pepper and Lemonade.
Customer: I'll have a diet pina colada with a pink . . . no, wait . . . blue umbrella in it.

On top of that, the employees at Busch Gardens are forced to wear the stereotypical, far-from-politically-correct clothing of the "nation" in which they work. My idea of a good job is just about any job in which I *don't* have to wear lederhosen.

These employees also have to listen to a non-stop recording of Swedish polka music which is only interrupted on the half-hour by the Big Band of Dutch Clog Dancers Ten Minute Extravaganza. Let me just say that if I worked at Ye Olde Waffle Cone Ice Cream Shoppe for more than fifteen minutes, I would stick my head in ye olde waffle iron.

Of course the basic point of an amusement park is to go stand in incredibly long lines to ride a roller coaster that lasts thirty seconds. I enjoy nothing more than paying forty dollars to stand in a tent with three hundred people who all think the line will go faster if they press up against my back so close that they start to complain my hair tastes funny.

Here are a few tricks I've learned that often get the people around you to give you a little room.

1. Suddenly double over and yell, "German sausage is coming back up!"
2. Turn to a friend and say, "It turns out that rash I have on my back is highly contagious after all."

3. Say to your friend, "You know, sometimes don't you
    feel like you could just crush the skull of the next
    person that bumps into you."
4. Rub back up against the person behind you and mut-
    ter, "Oh yeah." (warning: this can work well or com-
    pletely backfire.)

Just before I got on the ride, an announcement said
that all passengers wearing sandals needed to sit on them
during the ride. For those of you who haven't gone
through this experience, it really adds to the thrill of experiencing unnatural gravitational forces when there's a
pair of Birkenstocks lodged so far up your . . . Well, I
shouldn't go there. But let's just say I felt bad for the
women wearing sandals with heals.

Once I finally got my chance on the ride, I couldn't
help but wonder about the safety of some of these coasters. I realize employees come check every shoulder re-
straint when you get in the ride, but for some reason I
didn't want to put my life in the hands of a sixteen-year-
old wearing socks pulled up over his pants and shoes
with buckles. The tattoo of the bloody skull on his neck
didn't help either. I guess the park owners expect us to
think, "Well, if lederhosen-clad Billy lightly tugged on my
restraints, then of course I'm ready to be flipped upside
down at seventy miles an hour. Seriously, if that teenager with the hangover getting paid minimum wage says
it's safe, then let's go!"

The truth is if I saw a man in lederhosen walk up to
me on the street, I would probably yell, "Not this time,
creep!" and spray him with mace. But maybe that's just
me.

After the ride, my friends and I ate lunch and realized
that Busch Gardens is under the impression that their
authentic European food was actually imported from Eu-

rope despite the fact it was made in a plant in Pittsburgh for three cents a pound. We parkgoers end up selling our closest of kin just to be able to afford a hamburger, and we have to throw in a new car if we want cheese on that.

Anyway, as I staggered out of the park that afternoon eighty dollars lighter and slightly disoriented, there was a smile on my face. It was not because I had necessarily enjoyed myself, but simply because an employee had run up to me and yelled, "Thanks for coming," and I sprayed him with mace.

Mardi Gras: Topless Women Make The World Go Round

A week ago two friends and I went to New Orleans to enjoy the festivities of Mardi Gras. That's right, we drove thirty-two hours to spend forty-eight hours at our destination. Did we have a good time? Yes. Am I mentally unstable? Certainly.

We saw all the noteworthy sights of New Orleans – Jackson Square, the trolley cars, the Super Dome and half-naked women (not necessarily in that order of importance).

However, before my friends and I were able to view those sights, we had to endure a sixteen-hour car trip. There are certain things one must realize about being crammed in a Jeep Cherokee with two other guys for a long period of time. First, no matter how you position yourself in the back seat, you will always end up with your knee in your mouth. Secondly, whenever you try to go to sleep, the one guy who actually likes 'N Sync will decide it's time to blast "Bye, Bye, Bye." (The ironic thing is that no matter how many times 'N Sync sings "Bye,

Bye, Bye," they never freakin' go away!) The truth is, much to my horror, both of the guys I was with like 'N Sync. Needless to say, I've never come so close to jumping out of a moving vehicle.

The most interesting part of the car trip was stopping at little towns in the middle of Alabama and Mississippi. Strange things go on in those towns. We stopped at a place called The Omelet Shoppe at 4:30 in the morning. I'm pretty sure the only reason they spell it "shoppe" is not to appear old-timey, but rather because they simply don't know how to spell "shop."

In this establishment at 4:30 a.m., we actually saw a family with a three-year-old. I was thinking, "She's three years old! Let her go to bed! I'm sure she did not choose to be in The Omelet Shoppe in the middle of the night. Less omelets, more sleep!" But I didn't say that because I don't like to tell others how to raise their kids and also because this particular family had three guns on a rack inside their truck.

Following a full night of driving, we arrived at my friend's house where we were staying, and slept for an entire half hour before waking up to go out on the town. We didn't drink much but were extremely wasted from sleep deprivation anyway.

For those of you who don't know, Mardi Gras consists of millions of people drinking a hell of a lot while the men give the women beads to lift up their shirts.

The main method for men to obtain these beads is to grab them as women throw them out from balconies above the streets. So here's the formula of Mardi Gras in a nifty flow chart:

Girls throw beads to guys >> guys throw beads back to girls >> girls lift their shirts >> guys yell and drool like monkeys with brain damage >> repeat.

It's a vicious cycle, and if continued uninterrupted can last for years. The only way to stop it is to convince a woman to run naked down the street so all the men will chase her several miles into the Gulf of Mexico.

I find it strange that no matter how many times guys see a topless woman, we still go crazy about it. Most guys have seen bare-chested women in one form or another thousands of times, yet the second a shirt gets pulled up, we stand there like we've just come across the lost city of Atlantis. We go into shock. We stand in a catatonic state in fear that if we move we might wake up from the wonderful dream.

Women may wonder why the guys at Mardi Gras don't take off some of their clothes. Well, some do, but it's less common (thank God). I think the explanation for this is that women don't need a special event to see guys naked, all they have to do is ask.

Situation 1:

Guy: Show me your chest.
Girl: What will you give me?
Guy: These ten dollar beads.
Girl: Deal. (lifts shirt up)

Situation 2:

Girl: Show me your—
Guy: Will do! (rips off all his clothes)
Girl: What the hell? I was gonna say, "Show me your I.D."

Let me speak briefly to those of you who feel Mardi Gras is a sexist, obscene event. You're probably right. However, in defense of the celebration, I must say I don't think it would be taking place if there weren't women willingly participating. It just wouldn't be quite as exciting if it was like,

Jim: Hey Bill, show me your breasts!
Bill: Wooooo! (pulls up shirt)
Jim: Never mind! Cover them back up, for the love of God!

Another reason Mardi Gras isn't really sexist is because the women actually have an incredible amount of power over the men. On numerous occasions I saw hundreds of men worshipping one or two women. The women probably could have gotten the men to do whatever they wanted. Most of the girls only asked for beads, but I'm sure they could have gotten the guys to clean their apartments or buy them television sets just as easily.

Another interesting aspect of Mardi Gras is despite the screaming mobs of half-naked people carrying alcoholic beverages, the police were watching in amusement. Just about everything appears to be legal at Mardi Gras with the exception of anything moral and going to the bathroom on the sidewalks. I actually read that ninety percent of the arrests during Mardi Gras are for public urination.

Apparently public nudity, sexual harassment, public drunkenness, underage drinking, underage gambling and violence are all legal and often encouraged, but peeing on an already revolting, trash-covered sidewalk is terms for immediate arrest. Good to know the New Orleans police are making themselves useful.

So that's all that really happened at Mardi Gras. Oh yeah, I had a short run as a New Orleans prostitute, but that's not worth getting into right now.

A Broken Ankle, A Stolen Car
and A Partridge in A Pear Tree

During the last holiday season, I went home to see my family in hopes that several calamities would occur supplying me with material for future comedy writings. My family was happy to cooperate.

To begin with my younger brother broke his ankle. When I inform the average person that this happened, they inevitably want to know, "Who are you, and why are standing so close to me?" But next they ask how my brother broke his ankle.

Well, my brother was playing a very physical game of football, and right after throwing the game winning touchdown pass, he was knocked to the ground by several members of the Denver Bronco's defensive line. At that point he paused the Nintendo 64 video game and (I'm not making this next part up) attempted a standing front flip. He landed it, but broke his ankle in the process. In an incredible moment of courage, he found the composure to bow to the judge, which happened to be our black lab. She gave him a low score anyway.

Next, the power in our house went out for several days due to an ice storm. The ice storm caused our power to go out because ice accumulated on tree branches causing many of them to crash to the ground. When that happened, our power company turned off the electricity of random houses for the hell of it. With the lights and heat off, our house quickly took on the characteristics of the hull of a sinking ship-it was dark, cold and you could hear periodic yells of "Water starboard!," but those just came from the clinically insane man that lives somewhere in our basement.

After three days of living a chilling, dark existence, we were able to kidnap a power company employee and force him to restore our electricity. As far as I can tell he did this by staring up at the power lines and using several of his tools to scratch himself for two hours.

Once our electricity came back on, our refrigerator began malfunctioning. For some reason it stopped cooling completely, but on the plus side it was suddenly capable of making a great apple turnover. We tried to fix it ourselves at first, but it was evident that no matter how much time we put into it and no matter how many tools we used, no amount of scratching ourselves was going to solve this problem.

We called the closest General Electric service facility, which was located five minutes east of Nigeria. Over the phone we listened to a recording that said something like this: "Thanks for calling General Electric, if you would like to order a General Electric appliance, press one. To disconnect this call, press two. If you have a complaint, press two. For anything else, press two. Thank you."

After awhile we coerced a GE repairman into coming to our house. He asked to be known only as Technician 147, but I have a sneaking suspicion he was either a robot or Pauly Shore. He seemed to have the same amount of knowledge concerning refrigerator repair as I assume Pauly Shore has. It took a week and a half before the refrigerator was repaired, mainly because Technician 147 accidentally hooked up the ice dispenser to our cat which had actually died two years prior.

The final holiday calamity was that my older brother's car was stolen. It was stolen in Oklahoma, which happens to be rated number one in car theft among states shaped like frying pans. After my brother got over the initial disbelief and hours of saying to himself, "Think, where did I last have it?!," he rented a car and came home to Virginia. Three days after the theft we received a call at one in the morning. My younger brother answered the phone and (I'm not making this up) immediately ran to inform my dad that a *fleece* department in Oklahoma wanted to speak to him. It took quite awhile for my dad to figure out he was actually speaking to the Oklahoma *Police* Department. They told him that my brother's car had been recovered. The police said they would search the seat cushions for loose change and then return the car.

Despite all these annoyances some good things did happen to my family. For example my younger brother got a Bonsai tree as a gift, and he really loves it. A Bonsai tree is a small plant that if taken care of correctly for years and continuously tended to, may, under some circumstances, resemble a normal plant. Although it is a close relative to the Chia Pet, owning a Bonsai Tree in no way justifies shouts of "Ch-Ch-Ch-Chia!"

Yet, shouts of "Ch-Ch-Ch-Chia!" do justify the thorough beating of the person shouting. It is a vicious cycle which some believe is responsible for the extinction of the dinosaurs as well as this column . . .

Run for Cover! The Nudists Are Coming

After reading some of this book, I'm sure one question is resonating in your mind with great intensity. That question is, "Why haven't we heard anything about nude beaches?" Well fair readers, I don't want to disappoint you, so here's the story of my nude beach experience from this past summer.

One of the beaches I visited on a vacation this past summer ended up being a nude beach. This sounds exciting, doesn't it? The answer is – No, no, no, no, no. Most nude beaches are nasty. This is because a human being's desire to take off his or her clothes in a public place is directly proportional to his or her age times ugliness. Ninety-five percent of the people on a nude beach will make you wish real life had those black squares they have on public television. I actually tried to buy some black squares at the local store so that I could distribute them, but they were sold out.

While I was on this beach, I had to wonder why it's only beaches that have naked areas. I guess it's because we want to impress those few areas of the body that don't get to see the light of day much. So when we bring them out to chill for an extended period of time, we want it to be in an exotic location. We want them to come out, see this beautiful island in the Caribbean and say to themselves, "Wow, what a gorgeous beach! This guy really has something going here!"

It just wouldn't work if we were naked at other places. If there were nude subway cars, I think those parts of our body we wanted to impress would be like, "What the hell is this?

What's that smell? Put your pants back on! Cover me back up, for God's sake!"

Back to my traumatic experience: There were so many nasty people lounging around that I felt bad for the beach. What a terrible way to ruin a beautiful, exotic location. Mankind has certainly destroyed exotic places in other ways – construction, fires, oil spills. But I think the cruelest way is with the use of fat, ugly, naked people. I bet the natives on the island talk about it like it was a natural disaster. "Yeah, it was a beautiful beach . . . until last summer when the nakeds hit. It was devastating. We had to board up our windows, and my uncle's blind now."

One strange thing was that outside the nude beach I saw a sign that said, "No video taping or photography allowed." Do the people who put this sign up really think tourists are going to go to a nude beach to take family photos? That would spice up the old Christmas card, wouldn't it? "Honey, the Wilsons sent us a Christmas card . . . It looks like there's a fat, naked couple in the background. Do you think they're trying to tell us something?"

So like I said, ninety-five percent of the people on this nude beach were not enjoyable to look at. However, there was another five percent that almost made the trip worth while. And it's not just that there were a few attractive naked women on the beach. I've seen plenty of attractive, naked women before (in magazines). But the thing that got me was that there were attractive, naked women doing athletic activities such as paddleball. I wasn't the only one staring. Every man for a half mile radius couldn't bring himself to look away. If those girls hadn't eventually left, I would still be on that beach right now.

And watching attractive naked women is like a drug— after it's over you go into withdrawal. I wandered around for the next several days hoping to find more sexy naked women, but like I said, there weren't that many. Eventually I did get to see some more naked women playing paddleball, but it's not the same when they're eighty years old. Plus it was a little embarrassing to have to pay them to take their clothes off, and this was just yesterday in Barnes and Noble.

Even though there were a few attractive women on the beach, I can't imagine actually asking out a woman on a nude beach. It seems like when you're both naked already, you're beginning with everything out on the table. She's naked, you're naked, there's nowhere left to go. Normally it takes days, weeks, or even months to get to that point with a woman, depending on how drunk you both are. There's usually planning involved, calculations, dinners, gifts. But in the case of the nude beach, it's already done. Then once you do go out to dinner with this woman, she'll have clothes on. You will have taken several steps backward. You're losing ground. On the bright side though, I guess that is a good thing to have in common on a first date—the fact that you both enjoy taking your clothes off. That is probably more likely to get you asked up to his or her apartment than if the common ground is that you both enjoy backgammon.

So I decided to keep my clothes on, but I encountered awkward situations nonetheless. At one point I was sitting on the beach, and a naked guy was standing nearby. Suddenly he started up with the small talk. That's when I realized that small talk has no point when one person is nude. Eventually it's all gotta' come back to that fact that they're naked. You can't avoid it.

Naked Guy: How ya doing?
Me: Uh . . . fine. How about you?
Naked Guy: Pretty good. Beautiful day.
Me: Yeah, . . . so you're naked.
Naked Guy: Yeah. . . . The water's pretty nice today.
Me: Listen, you're still naked. We'll have to pick this up some other time.

Overall my trip to the nude beach was quite traumatic and to this day I get disoriented whenever I so much as hear the word "paddleball."

8

Fashion & Trends

Big Pants Aren't Just for People with Big Asses Anymore

There is a major entity overtaking the continental United States, and if we don't find a way to stop it soon, we will all suffocate under a blanket of denim and khaki. I am referring to nothing other than big pants.

It started as something simple enough. In 1990 a Midwest teenager named Earl wore his father's pants to school because all his other pants were currently being eaten by the family goat. It was a tough time for the family, and their goat had recently switched from tin cans to denim in an attempt to lose weight. At school Earl's friends initially made fun of him with clever insults such as, "Your pants are big," and "You must have gotten those pants from someone bigger than you." However, over time the other children realized that if they too wore looser pants they would not feel like they were being molested all day, at least as long as they weren't in Mr. Herbert's math class. Soon enough all the kids began wearing their father's pants (forcing all the fathers in the town to wear their daughters' clothes).

Unfortunately big pants are now present in every household in America with the possible exception of the Amish ones, but it's only a matter of time. I must admit that I too have been drawn in by the craze. While I don't wear pants that could house a professional sumo wrestler and his family, I do occasionally wear pants or shorts that could house a professional sumo wrestler's slightly overweight dog. I'm not proud of this fact, but I think we're all happy to distance ourselves from the decade of spandex known as the 80's.

After big pants were well established, the young adults of America got together and decided that there still was not enough denim and cotton draped from their bodies, so they came up with cargo pants. I too wear cargo pants, and I too don't know why I'm doing it. I try my hardest to find some "cargo" to put in the pockets in order to at least make it functional clothing. I never thought marsupials would lead the way in the fashion world. If we humans also raised our young in pouches that extended from our bodies, cargo pants would make a lot more sense. Sometimes I keep a squirrel in one of the pockets just to put my mind at ease.

I don't claim to understand fashion. I just found out last week that white powdered wigs aren't cool anymore. However, I've finally figured out how to stay on top of fashion trends. I have obtained the holy grail of the fashion world. The answer is: Ask a carpenter. Face it, carpenters have lead the way in many of the recent clothing trends. Long before it was cool for teenagers to wear their pants around their knees, who do you think was showing off the most crack? The carpenter. Long before we were sporting the meaningless hammer loop on our pants, who do you think had one? The carpenter. The latest trend is to buy pants that already look like they've been worn for several years. Who do you think has been wearing the same pair of nasty pants for several years? The carpenter.

I want to know how the companies get pants to have the already-worn look to them. Maybe they have professional pant wearers – guys that just walk around in a room all day wearing a new pair of jeans. I think we consumers should get a little I.D card with our jeans, telling us about the man that has worn our pants for several months. "Your pant wearer's name is Jim. He's a Gemini from Chicago and says that if you knew what he enjoyed doing in his spare time, you would not want to wear these pants anymore."

And how pathetic is it that those of us who can afford nice, brand new pants are buying pants that look old and used? Do you know what a homeless person would give to have a new pair of pants? Do you? Well, I don't know either, but I bet it would be something cool.

By the way people, I encourage you to look deep down in your hearts and your pants and think about the thousands of homeless people in America who are forced to wear pants that actually fit. If we all just gave a little bit of fabric we could help put thousands of people in huge pants right away. We could also use some of the fabric to build denim houses. Just think, your pants could be someone else's home, preferably not at the same time. Seriously, just a cargo pocket a month can make a difference. Think about it.

I'd Like A Short Grande with A Gimpy Leg

With the sudden ubiquity of coffee, coffee shops, coffee houses and coffee ice cream in our society, we the consumers find ourselves asking one question, "How many times am I going to burn my tongue before I realize that coffee is as hot as %#$*?!"

Coffee is the only food product I can think of which is extremely painful to consume until several minutes after it has been purchased. You don't see any cantaloupes that are fatally poisonous for the first five minutes after you buy them. I've also never been to the grocery store and heard the cashier say, "Remember, you might want to wait a couple of minutes before you eat that Twinkie or it will release a toxin that will melt your teeth and jaw into a puddle. Thank you, come back soon."

Because the coffee is so hot, most coffee shops now have protectors for the coffee cups – a circular piece of cardboard that you slide over the cup so that you don't burn your hands. The idea behind these cardboard protectors is that the coffee is so hot, it's even too hot to hold without something around the cup. If the coffee is that hot, why the hell are we pouring this scalding liquid down our throats? I want to see the answer to that question on *Who Wants to Be A Millionaire?*

Regis: Oh, I'm sorry Sam, but the correct answer was "Because we're incompetent caffeine-craving morons who don't care if we burn holes through our tracheas. But thanks for playing, and good luck moving out of your mother's basement. That's all for tonight folks. This is Regis Pilbin . . . saying I like . . . dramatic . . . pauses . . . and goodnight."

Why do we as a nation suddenly have this need for so much caffeine anyway? We must just be a tired nation, which is pretty disturbing since we're only two hundred and twenty-five years old. If we're this tired already, I feel bad for Europe. England must be on crack by now. And that's probably why Holland legalized drugs – they needed something to keep them going after all these years. That also explains why some legalized drugs in Holland are sold in coffee shops – it's the natural progression of things. I'm sure there's a lot of people who will be happy when Starbucks starts offering herbal tea with a different kind of herb or mocha crackuccinos.

But I always feel a little awkward in coffee shops. I think it's because they've invented this whole separate language that you have to speak to order anything. I mean, you can't just order regular coffee anymore. Regular coffee doesn't exist. You have to pick between grandes, lattes, cappuccinos and frappuccinos. My problem is when I hear "Frappuccino," I don't think, "type of coffee drink." I hear "Frappuccino," I think, "professional killer." If I'm introduced to a Mr. Frappuccino, I keep my distance.

Then, for the sizes of the drinks, you have to choose between "short," "tall" or "grande." What is this? Are we ordering midgets? "I'd like the short grande with the gimpy leg. Yeah, that's him. Whoa, he's a quick one."

So I recently went into a coffee shop and planned to sound like I had some idea of what I was talking about. I ordered a regular coffee grande. That went fine. Then I actually caught myself saying, "And leave a little room at the top for cream and sugar." That's when I thought, "Leave a little room at the top?! What the hell does that mean? 'No, I'd like you to leave a little room at the bottom, please. Right there under the coffee. I want to inject my cream and sugar down there. Thanks." Moral of the story: I'm an idiot.

Back to the topic—Coffee's gotten incredibly expensive too. I paid three dollars for some coffee the other day. What about coffee could possibly cost that much? It's just coffee bean and hot water. Do Juan Valdez and his donkey come with the coffee? Because if not, I want some money back.

Overall, I think coffee shops are just too cozy for me. You feel a need to sit and chat, and then if you stay there too long, you start writing weird-ass jazz poetry. It's dangerous. It should say on each cup, "Warning: Excessive time in coffee shop could cause extreme cases of weird-ass jazz poetry." If they had that warning, it would put a stop to tragic scenes like this one.

Tammy: How was your day?
James: Pretty good. I just hung out here in the coffee shop all day. But anyway, . . . today was like butterflies that . . . fly away.
Tammy: Was that weird-ass jazz poetry?
James: Oh God! It's happening!
Bongo Player: Relax, it's natural.
Tammy: Where'd the bongo player come from?
James: He's been following me around. I think I accidentally

paid for him with the coffee. Why else would it cost three dollars?

For All Your Hair Cutting
and Mounted Bass Needs

A couple of weeks ago I decided to get my hair cut at a nearby Hair Cuttery. One of my friends warned me, "Don't go there. Those hair stylists probably just got out of styling school." I laughed at this cautionary remark because for most of my life I've been frequenting a much worse barber shop in Virginia. In order to protect the guilty, I'll refer to my old barber as Larry.

Larry is not exactly a "hair stylist," and I doubt he went to "styling school." He probably doesn't even have a "hair cutting license," and he certainly does not have "good hygiene" in the traditional sense. However, he can kill a ten-point buck with only a spork.

Most professional offices have diplomas or licenses on the wall. On the other hand, Larry's major qualification appears to be a mounted stuffed raccoon that must have delved into the wrong trash can. (Keep in mind that all this is frighteningly true.) Many popular hair styling places have pictures of beautiful people on the walls. Larry has pictures of himself holding up bass. I'm not quite sure how those are supposed to help me get a hair cut. "Um, can you cut my hair like that bass on the wall. I like how he's got his bangs." Other than that, there are approximately three hundred and forty-six go-cart racing trophies surrounding the room that seem to say, "I may not know how to cut hair, but I sure can drive a go-cart!"

There is also a prominently displayed calendar that features nearly naked women standing next to sports cars. This is not surprising considering the fact that in this barbershop most of the employees' number one fantasy is to see a woman making love to some sort of motor vehicle.

There is only one haircut that Larry gives as far as I can tell. It's called the "summer cut," and it is a lot like the haircut you would get from a Flowbee on strong acid. So this brings me to my point that I wasn't afraid to go to the Hair Cuttery because I was accustomed to having Larry pull my hair out with rusty scissors.

When I first entered this cuttery of hair, there were no other customers, and the woman turned to me and said, "How can I help you." As far as I could tell, I was standing in a small room used for nothing other than cutting hair. Would I have come to the Hair Cuttery for anything other than a haircut? Stunned like a convict deer in a police searchlight, I responded, "I'd like an erotic cake, please."

When it was finally worked out that I did indeed desire a haircut, she asked how I wanted it cut. I've always hated this part of the haircut because I have no idea how to describe the shape of hair. I usually end up saying, "Well . . . I want it trimmed sorta' short, but not really short, but still short, just not too short. I mean, I want it to take awhile to grow back, because I don't want to be back here anytime soon. . . . Well, can you make me look like Brad Pitt? I don't mean the hair. I just want my face to look like his. Can you do that? Forget it, just cut it all off."

In this particular instance, however, I decided to be very precise. I said, "Just trim it and take about a half an inch off the front." I'm not really sure what a half an inch is in hair terms, and apparently the woman cutting my hair had absolutely no idea either. Before I knew it, staring back at me in the mirror was a good old summer cut.

My horrible haircut was not a freak mistake either. It's happened to me more than once, and it's come to my attention that other customers would prefer the drugged up Flowbee over returning to this particular Hair Cuttery.

I think this Hair Cuttery should not try so hard to be a presentable hair cutting facility. The employees should just stick some bass and raccoons up on the walls because no one expects a good haircut from a place with dead animals on the walls.

"I got a terrible haircut today."

"Where'd you go?"

"That place with the dead raccoon on the wall. I really thought they would do a good job."

9

Men & Women

Men and Women Go Together
Like Peas and Cantaloupe

The other day a female friend of mine came to me for advice about guys. This seems to be a common tactic for women. If women are having problems with a guy, they will attack a different guy for the answers, much like velociraptors; except velociraptors rarely had relationship problems. Then, if another girl walks in on the interrogation, she'll help the first girl, and they'll work as a team to slowly break the guy down. Girls somehow know what the other members of their team are driving at, and they'll help each other out. They can even explain the actions of the rest of the members. Guys, on the other hand, have a loose bond among one another but don't really keep track of what the other guys are doing. The only thing that keeps us together is if one guy scores, we'll chalk that up as a point for the whole team. Other than that, there's not much sharing of information going on. This is why girls go to the bathroom in groups and guys go alone.

So my friend wanted me to explain why guys never

see the "signs" that women give out to guys they're attracted to, and I told her the truth. I told her the blatant truth which is difficult for many women to accept. The truth is that men don't know what the hell's going on. Ladies, give up on the signs, the signals, the hints, the clues, the gestures, the indications and even the body language. We're not gonna' get it. "Oh, you offered him a stick of gum? Well, my God! How could anyone not pick up on that piece of key evidence?!" (I hope the sarcasm in that last sentence was overly evident.)

Girls, you could make a giant highway sign that says "Ask Me Out!" and smack the guy over his head with it so hard it leaves an imprint on his forehead, and he still wouldn't get it. You could have people with neon orange batons directing him toward you and Boys II Men in your living room singing "I'll Make Love to You," and he would still think you just wanted to be friends.

But these rules only apply for most girls. If there is a girl that a guy is incredibly interested in, then the guy will become Sherlock Holmes all of a sudden. He will start finding clues in everything.

Guy #1: There she is over at that table. See how she just took that bite of food, she wants me.
Guy #2: Are you sure?
Guy #1: Yeah, she's trying to look seductive. And last week when I introduced myself, all she did was ask me how I knew where she lived. She didn't call the police or anything!

Another problem is that women always think they're seeing bad signs. They say things like, "Oh my God. He didn't e-mail me when we were both online the other day. He must hate me!" My response to this is, "It's not that he hates you. He probably didn't notice you were online because he was busy downloading hardcore porn." Or women say, "I passed him on the sidewalk, and he didn't stop to talk to me." To this I say, "It's not that he didn't want to talk to you. He was probably in a rush to go download hardcore porn." Seriously women, give guys the benefit of the doubt.

I have also heard several girls say they don't want to flirt with a guy they like because they don't want the guy to think they're too eager. Ladies, we guys are having a hard enough time figuring women out without the added confusion of your eagerness games. No guy has ever turned a girl down because she was "too eager." In the history of the world, the following conversation has never taken place.

Guy #1: Hey Bill, today I met a supermodel who is incredibly nice, enjoys nude beaches, beer and football, and says she is completely in love with me. I have never met a sweeter, more gorgeous woman. Unfortunately, I had to turn her down.
Guy #2: Why?!
Guy #1: She was too eager. I can't have that.

Attempting to get men and women to understand each other is about as easy as teaching quantum physics to a muskrat with attention deficit disorder. I don't think men and women will ever really figure each other out, but we should never give up. . . . Wait, never mind, I was thinking of something else. We should give up.

That Beer Bottle Brings out Your Cheek Bones

I went shopping this week . . . with my girlfriend. For most men that sounds like the opening lines to a horror movie. Women are always saying they want their man to show more emotion. Well ladies, here's the answer. If you tell your guy that you want him to shop all day with you, you will finally see him weep like a little girl. And if you break the news during the final game of a best-of-seven series, you should make sure there aren't any guns in the house.

For a guy, shopping with a woman is slightly less fun than giving birth to a bag of rusty nails. Guys will do anything to avoid shopping. If we decide we need new jeans, we'll try to find other ways to get them without going to a store. We'll search E-Bay to see if anyone has a used pair of jeans up for sale. Or we'll begin wearing whatever we can find around the house. "Baggy is popular. I'll just wrap the drapes around me."

If all this fails, guys will finally go to a store, but we won't "shop." Shopping implies hours upon hours of looking at clothes. A guy will enter the store, grab the first pair of jeans in sight, and get the hell out of there – even if the jeans he grabbed were on another customer at the time.

Shopping with a woman is completely different. With women there is browsing, trying on, comparing prices, accessorizing and much more. There is no accessorizing for guys. Accessorizing for us is holding a beer.

Bubba: Jimmy, that beer bottle really brings out your cheek bones.
Jimmy: Thanks, Bubba. That mustard stain on your overalls just screams "let's have fun!"
Bubba: I'm so glad you think so because that's exactly what I was going for.

We don't even know what we're supposed to be doing while we're following a woman around. We just repeat, "Oh, that looks nice. You look slender in that," and pray that the next store has a couch. A couch in a women's clothing store is like an oasis in a desert. Any guy in a woman's clothing store will sell his soul for as much as a lawn chair.

Women constantly ask guys if certain outfits look good. Ladies, let me break it down for you once and for all. The official stand of the male race concerning women's clothing is: The less material, the better. The tighter, the better. Other than that, we have no opinion. Half the time, for all we can tell, you've tried on fourteen pairs of the exact same pants.

The only thing for a guy to do in a women's clothing store is stare at the pictures and the mannequins. Women, tell me why these mannequins are so hot? Half of them don't even have heads, but what a body! Ladies, if you want us to realize how good you look while you're trying on those clothes, stop putting the Playboy bunny mannequins all over the place. Otherwise this will continue to be the situation:

Woman: Sweetheart, how does this look?
Man: Uh, . . . actually Honey. I'm going home with the mannequin. Check out her rock hard ass. I think she works out.

Another reason being in a women's clothing store is so awkward for men is that the sales people always run up and say, "How can I help you?" This worries guys. We feel like we're being accused of something, so we quickly blurt out, "I'm with my girlfriend. She dragged me in here. I've never tried on women's clothing!" There's also the fact that we're outnumbered. We become frightened in a store with fifty women and two guys. And it's not just the numbers, it's the atmosphere too. The clothes, the wallpaper, the pictures, the smell. Everything's against us. If it was fifty women and two guys in a hot tub, we'd be perfectly happy.

On every shopping trip with a girlfriend, there also comes the point at which she wants to help the guy shop. This is bad news, but sometimes we get sucked into it. In any men's department store, at least half the men are being dragged around by girlfriends or wives.

The worst part is having to try things on. Guys don't try on. We'd rather buy it, take it home, wear it for a day, realize it's too tight, use it to wash our car and then let the dog have it. That's the trying-on process of a man. So if the guy gets forced into trying something on, he then has to go through the walk of shame from the dressing room out to the girlfriend. It's always a very slow, sad walk, maybe without shoes on. He finally gets to her, and she says, "Those are too big, right? Here's eight other pairs to try on, and some shirts that might go with them. I'll go see if I can find you some undies."

That's the point when the guy realizes he no longer even has a chance with the cute mannequin in the corner.

7 Failed Ad Campaigns

1. Child laborers made it, so if you don't buy one, you'll be disappointing *them*!
2. If it gives you a burning case of pink eye, we'll refund your money. No questions asked!
3. Won't chafe your ass . . . much
4. Tested on monkeys to make sure it works!
5. It's worked for people fatter than you! (This does not apply to people over 411 lbs.)
6. Sure, you could get something that works better, but who has that kind of time?
7. Our beer is so good, it will make former alcoholics realize what they're missing!

10

Miscellaneous

Whassup Pimp Dawg?!

Going back to work after a vacation can be quite depressing. You have to return to the same old desk, the same old conversations, the same old beer and the same old friends—if only you could remember their names. (I mean the friends, not the beers, but that's not to say that beer can't be your friend.)

Of course starting a new job is not much fun either. When beginning a new job, you tend to meet a lot of new and interesting people—They're just not interesting enough for you to remember who they are. I'm terrible with remembering people, and it's often embarrassing. For example one day I will be introduced to a nice girl named Susan. The next day I might see her again and mistake her for an automobile.

Sometimes I won't even remember people I know well.

Person: Lee!
Me: . . . Hey! How are you?
Person: I'm great. I've really missed you, Lee.

Me: Really?
Person: Of course!
Me: Oh. . . . Okay.
Person: Don't tell me you don't know who I am.
Me: Of course I do. You are . . . uh . . . hm. Didn't we go to high school together?
Person: Not quite.
Me: You must be Ed!
Person: No.
Me: Are you sure you aren't Ed?
Person: I'm your dad, Lee.
Me: Daaaaad! Well, your hair's shorter. I didn't recognize you. Besides, I haven't seen you in ages.
Person: Two weeks.
Me: Gosh, has it been that long?

One possibility for avoiding embarrassing moments such as this one is to have nicknames for people. Here is an extensive list that will be enough for you to survive any awkward conversation:

1. Tiger
2. Champ
3. Pimp Dawg

To demonstrate the effectiveness of these nicknames, allow me to convey a conversation I had a couple of days ago.

Person: Whassup, Lee?!
Me: Hey, Pimp Dawg!
(I don't remember the rest of the conversation because Pimp Dawg and his friends managed to pack my head into a small Tupperware container.)
While being introduced to all these new people, there is

also the problem of the mandatory fake conversations. During these you are forced to ask all the usual questions, "Where do you live?," "What do you like to do?," "If I poke you in the eye, will you please stop talking to me?" These conversations can get incredibly boring and are most likely the reason the Pilgrims left England. Unfortunately, these boring, mundane conversations found their way across the ocean.

I believe the best solution when you are faced with a pointless conversation is to act as if you are a reporter on a tightly-run television news program. Sure, it might cause some confusion at first, but I think it could solve many problems. For example, when a stranger continues to talk to you long after the proper introductions have been exchanged, you could abruptly interrupt the person and say, "Ohhhh, I'm sorry. That's all the time we have for today. I'll see you next time on News at Five!" Then you merely turn and walk away.

Another problem is the awkward silence during a conversation. However, the newscaster persona would easily solve this. As a newscaster, one is allowed to fire completely random questions at people because, after all, that is your job.

Example #1

You: . . . That's great.
Person: Yeah.
(Painfully awkward silence.)
You: Sources tell me that you are a boring, annoying, self-absorbed man. Is this true?
Person: What?! Who said that?!
You: I have sources that I can't reveal. Just answer the question.

Example #2

Person: So you have to understand that grain elevators are crucial in—
You: Do you enjoy dumping vanilla icing down your pants?
Person: What?! I thought we were talking about grain elevators.
You: I'm just reading off the cards here. The higher-ups want you to answer the question.
Person: You have cards?
You: I'll ask the questions. Back to the icing.
Person: Well, I have been known to partake in the icing down the pants now and again.
You: That's what I thought. That's all for News at Five! Now, stop talking to me.

Big Foot, Richard Simmons and Other Extraterrestrial Beings

We see them everyday – people that seem just a little unusual. You know the ones I mean. That lady that lives next door with the thirty-one cats. Or that guy that mows your lawn every Saturday even though you never asked him to and don't pay him. These unusual people bring up an obvious and very important question: Have aliens landed on earth? And if so, do the male aliens know not to stand too close to other men in public restrooms?

The constant fear of alien invasion has been on the minds of people ever since one man, Herbert Shuttlebaum, spotted the first unidentified flying object in 1898. Mr. Shuttlebaum reported that he was eating lunch with his wife when the object came out of nowhere, hit him in the face and then disappeared forever. He was shocked by the object's striking resemblance to a roast beef sandwich, including the strong smell of mayonnaise. A couple of years later Mr. Shuttlebaum admitted that the object was most likely his wife's roast beef sandwich, which she had thrown at him in a fit of anger. However, until his death in 1921 he never stopped asking, "If that was my wife's roast beef sandwich, then why was there no pickle? Tell me that! Why was there no pickle?!"

This single haunting incident was enough to spark a phenomenon. Ever since that day, UFO spottings have been more common than Las Vegas Elvis impersonators with no arms. People are seeing extraterrestrial beings in the sky, on the land and in their George Foreman grills. The frightening side of all this is that if it is discovered that even one of these thousands of people is right about what he or she saw, the following serge of made-for-TV movies would be unparalleled.

Another unexplainable incident occurred just three years ago. Ralph Henderson went to his family doctor to ask about a red discoloration on his chest. The doctor examined Mr. Henderson and stated that the redness was either due to an alien abduction in which the beings planted a tracking device inside him or the fact that this particular red area on Mr. Henderson was currently caught in his jacket zipper. For these past three years Mr. Henderson has tried to get his insurance company to pay for alien abduction treatment, but the company insists that the redness will go away if he just unzips his jacket. Yet, Mr. Henderson is positive he was abducted because ever since the time when he believes a tracking device was inserted in him, he has found himself uncontrollably attracted to overweight toll booth operators.

Could Mr. Henderson be right all along? If aliens do exist, we can't help but wonder how we should act toward them. Once they arrive on earth, there are several problems that must be solved. For example, should humans receive special treatment on public transportation? Would *Third Rock from The Sun* still be as lame as it is now? And would 1-800-COLLECT still be just ten cents a minute if you're calling a galaxy that is 7,000 light years away? (The commercials act like it's so simple, but I haven't heard the answer to that question.)

Getting humans and aliens to coexist peacefully may be harder than it seems. What if the aliens that arrive on earth are no larger than a fun-size candy bar? If that's the case, would these tiny aliens be available in pet stores, and how often would you have to change the newspaper in their cages? On the other hand what if the aliens are the size of monster trucks? Would they be allowed to travel on commercial airplanes, and if so, would their carry-on bags still have to fit in the overhead compartment?

Some people believe that these questions are pointless because they feel that aliens already inhabit earth and have blended seamlessly into our society in the same manner that the contents of a pina colada blend together. I personally can't accept this proposal because I can't comprehend why any alien being would choose to live on a planet that contains The Backstreet Boys. This theory, however, does provide a simple explanation to such mysteries as crop circles, the Bermuda Triangle, and how millions of Furbies were able to disappear off the face of the earth in seconds.

Yet the answers to other mysteries still elude mankind. Can anyone say with certainty what kinds of beings are the Loch Ness Monster, Big Foot and Richard Simmons? What caused these abnormal beasts to live the way they do? And couldn't "Sweating to The Oldies" be some sort of alien torture? Plus, we mustn't forget the mind-boggling Great Pyramids. The manner in which the mummies are buried in the Pyramids suggests that the Egyptians knew there would be better skincare products available in the future. Yet, why did the Egyptians not at least give the mummies a couple of Qtips for their long journey? Is there no earwax in the after life?

Obviously aliens must be involved somewhere in this crazy Rubik's Cube of mysteries, but this time we can't just peal the stickers off and put them back in the right place. Instead, we must tenaciously continue fiddling with the cube until we get extremely frustrated and crush it with a tack hammer. No one really knows where to find the answers to these mysteries, yet I believe we should look to the Magic Eight Ball for the answer.

Me: Magic Eight Ball, do alien beings inhabit the earth?
Eight Ball: For the love of God, would you stop jiggling me?! My prediction is . . . I'm about to vomit!

Airport Baggage Claim Found to Be Hotbed of Criminal Activity

This past summer I went on several airplane trips. I noticed a drastic problem on every trip – the well-known institution of baggage claim. I think we all need to admit that baggage claim is more than a few tweaks away from a perfect system. As long as there is an abundance of random luggage moving on conveyor belts, there always will be an abundance of deluded travelers picking up the wrong bags.

People tend to ignore whether a bag is actually theirs. It's always encouraging to hear the guy next to you at baggage claim saying, "I like this one, and this one, and . . . this one has wheels! Alright, I've got my bags. Let's go."

It is amazing how hysterical people get at baggage claim. Just hearing the word "baggage" seems to have a Pavlovian effect on most people, causing their adrenaline to surge and mouths to foam. Everybody always rushes up and tries to get a spot around the conveyor belt before all the good ones are taken. Some people go over to stand around other conveyer belts because they don't have the patience to wait for their own to start up. Perhaps they want to observe other travelers' techniques in order to improve their own baggage claim abilities. I have devised a different, very simple, foolproof process, which I will explain step-by-step.

1. Wait for *my* bags to come around the conveyor belt.
2. Pull my bags off the belt.

On the other hand, most people have a much more intricate, physically demanding process. For some reason, they try to look through the plastic curtain at the end of the belt. I don't know what they expect to see back there. Then, when they hear the belt motor start, their eyes get as big as Frisbees, they begin sweating with anticipation and their muscles tense in preparation for the grab. Finally, the suitcases come over the horizon. Everybody acts like if they don't get their luggage on its first time around, it will fall into a pit of baggage-devouring alligators. They're afraid that once it goes back behind those curtains, it may never come out again. People jump over and tackle each other like six-year-olds on "Free Tickle-Me-Elmo Day" at Toys R Us. Old women get knocked down left and right. It's every man for himself. Survival of the fittest. Natural selection occurs before your eyes. This kind of thing is way beyond what Darwin could have imagined. Shouts can be heard from all directions. "That's ours, John! Get it! It's almost to the curtain! Dive, John! Dive!!"

Why is everybody so eager to get their suitcase anyway? It's a bag mostly full of underwear, miniature bottles of shampoo and sweat pants. Yeah, you might want to pick it up some time, but it's not like it's your children on the belt. Of course, there occasionally are children going around the conveyor belts, but that's beside the point.

Even the suitcases are usually worth more than their contents. They have fancy wheels and handles and pockets and pouches and zippers. A lot of them are more technologically advanced than my car, not to mention capable of going faster. Many of these suitcases have incredibly useful features, like pockets inside other pockets. Maybe the inner pockets are just there so that the outer pockets will have a place to put their hands.

In order to understand fully the extensive problems with baggage claim, we first must figure out why people take the wrong bags. The majority of the people seem to have no idea which suitcase is theirs even though they spent the entire month of July packing it. I always hear people saying, "I can never tell which one's mine. They all look alike." I'm sure the suitcases are going around the belt, looking up at all the exasperated human faces, and saying to each other,

"I can never tell which one's mine. They all look alike." The problem is that people get so excited during the baggage claim process that they simply grab every suitcase that looks remotely like theirs and hurry home to enjoy their apparent success. Because people do this, I usually end up having to take home someone else's suitcase containing whips, assorted leather bondage, whipped cream and a "Girls of The ACC" *Playboy* because somebody unknowingly fled the airport with my suitcase full of *Simpsons* merchandise and a "Girls of The ACC" *Playboy*.

So, my advice for the next time you travel on an airplane is be patient, make sure the luggage you claim is yours and when you're told to put your tray table up, do it! It saves lives!

Fun with Small Explosives

No matter when you're reading this, I'm sure some big celebration is coming up soon. Christmas, Mardi Gras, Groundhog's Day, Arbor Day, Tropical Drink Appreciation Day, etc. Right when we finish with one, there's another one coming. No matter where you look, it seems there is always some holiday bearing down on you like that giant boulder in that movie in which Indiana Jones raids that lost ark. I forget the name.

But the truth is I like celebrations because more often than not they include music, dancing and if I'm feeling especially saucy, pulling up my shirt. My favorite part about any big celebration is the possibility of fireworks. I've been setting off fireworks for as long as I can remember. I believe I actually threw some Snap & Pops when I was only a fetus, but I've moved on to more dangerous explosives since then.

There is something about fireworks that mercilessly attracts both boy and man alike. Because they are illegal in Virginia, as a kid I only got a glimpse of them when my family would go on vacation to states in which the number one export was devices with fuses, namely North Carolina.

During these trips, I would look out the window of the car as we cruised down the highway of an unfamiliar land and allow my little mind to be over-stimulated by the vast array of multicolored firecracker billboards until my little stomach would become over-stimulated with car sickness, resulting in a not-so Happy Meal all over the back seat of the car.

I believe those billboards are not much different from the Sirens which beckoned Odysseus and his men to join them on the deadly rocks. In the same manner firecrackers seem to beckon men to join them in enjoying flammable chaos.

Firecrackers have several crucial elements which make them irresistible to most boys and men.

1. They bring out man's primal instinct to dance around a blazing fire like an idiot.
2. They can do damage to less manly objects such as fat-free cookies and boy band posters.
3. They have godless yet sexy images on the packages such as she-devils.
4. They are illegal enough to be fun, yet not so illegal that the law against them includes the phrase "two consecutive life sentences."
5. They are dangerous enough that if something goes wrong you could lose a finger, but not so dangerous that if something goes wrong you could lose a nephew.

My dad understood a boy's need for firecrackers, so he would let me and my brothers purchase a few every once in awhile. We would stop at some run-down shack that boasted the goods. The shack was always run by a man with a name like "Short-Fuse McGee" or "One-Eyed Jed." We tried not to let that affect our overall enthusiasm.

Although my mom predictably sought to limit the number of explosive devices we purchased, she never succeeded. My dad tried to act as a voice of reason with advice such as, "If you set the neighbor's cat on fire, I'm not helping you put it out."

Of course my brothers and I inevitably went straight to the biggest firecracker in the store. We went for the one that looked as if Jed had made it himself in his back yard, the one that might well have been used by Iraqi troops to combat NATO missiles, the one that had a warning label that simply read, "Do not activate this device unless you're stupid." That's the one.

Because my dad wanted to continue to have three living sons, he never let us buy "the big one," but we did spend enough money on firecrackers to put two of Jed's kids through professional wrestling college.

Usually we'd wait until we got home to begin lighting fuses, but sometimes we couldn't hold out that long. So we'd set off a couple of perfectly innocent bottle rockets in the parking lot of the store with Jed cheering us on. It was during one such episode that a man writing an article on the definition of "white trash" came and took our picture.

Over the next couple months, my brother and I would light various firecrackers in our driveway. We soon discovered that it was rather amusing to blow up food products. (This is one of the greatest discoveries an eight-year-old can make.) I actually remember going into 7-11 and buying snacks specifically to blow them up.

I truly remember thinking, "What will look good exploding? Focus! If this pastry were blown to pieces, would it look cool? Would blueberry or cherry cream filling be more flammable?" My life has never been more like *Southpark*.

Eventually we ran out of fireworks and our destructive

tendencies were tamed—
    much to the relief of woodland creatures for miles around.
Then we went out and purchased a pellet gun.

7 Super Heroes You'll Never See

1. Not-so Super Man
2. The Bland Ranger
3. Racial Epithets Girl
4. The Incredible Mr. Contagious
5. Full Frontal Nudity Guy
6. The Sexual Avenger
7. King of Cottage Cheese

Bathroom Humor

To all my faithful readers (all three of you): So far in this book we've had some good times ("Big Foot, Richard Simmons and Other Extraterrestrial Beings") and some bad times ("Elvis Fathered My Hamsters"). During the course of our relationship, I knew there would come a time when I would have to resort to bathroom humor. That greatly feared time is now upon us. So if you're still with me (both of you), let's explore the repulsive world of the public bathroom. But I must warn you that the following may not be suitable for women, children and some types of cheeses.

    The public bathroom is the king of all nastiness. It's Mardi-Gras for diseases and sicknesses and everybody's invited. So why are we so adamant about locking ourselves in these cubes of nastiness? First thing we do when we get in a stall is make sure the lock works. We don't want to be able to escape from that disease-culturing cubicle too easily.

When we go into a stall that doesn't lock, we come up with the craziest ways to make sure people don't come in. We become MacGyver, rigging makeshift locks out of toothpicks and toilet water. We've got our bodies contorted to brace for the person we know is going to attack us while we're on the toilet. The reason we're so worried is because we would hate to die on the toilet seat. That would be too embarrassing. All the people would come to see the crime scene and stare at the chalk outline with the pants around the ankles. If someone tried to kill us while we were on the toilet, we would probably be like, "I don't care if you kill me, just let me zip up my pants!"

(For any women reading this, I can say with confidence that this next part, well, you just won't understand.) The urinals are just as disgusting as the stalls. My problem at the urinals is that I never know where to look when I'm standing there facing the wall. I mean, you can't look down, can't look to your left or right because you've usually got other guys there. A lot of the time urinals even have those dividers between each one in case someone's tempted to cheat. It's a little bit like *Jeopardy!*

You also can't look straight forward because there's always some sort of nasty spot on the wall or obscene graffiti. (Figuring out those lewd pictures drawn on the walls is impossible. You're saying to yourself, "What is that? I don't think that position is possible. There are too many legs. I'll write down this number here and get some answers.") Urinals would be a lot better if there were little televisions implanted in the wall so guys would have something to look at. The problem is that if we had that, we'd never leave. That's a guy's ultimate fantasy—to be able to watch television and not have to get up to go to the bathroom.

In any given public bathroom there are essentially two types of toilet paper. First, there is the incredibly painful, rock-hard, absorption-qualities-of-saran-wrap type of toilet paper. That kind feels like you're using a two by four. I don't see why the manufacturers even go to the trouble of making it resemble toilet paper. They might as well just supply us with a box of aluminum siding right there in stall.

The other type of toilet paper is so thin that it has more spiritual qualities than actual physical ones. It's thinner than Kate Moss sucking in, and it just sort of disintegrates in your hands. It serves no purpose. It's really just there for moral support.

I find it pathetic that some people take this almost nonexistent toilet paper and put it down on the toilet seat to protect them from the disease-fest that is the public bathroom. "Nothing will be able to penetrate this rock-solid wall of loosely woven paper strands."

And guys, here's my parting words of advice. If at all possible, avoid using the urinal directly next to another guy. Whenever men have their pants unzipped, it's safe to say that you need to give them some room. There should always be a little extra space or somebody's going to get hurt.

New Humor Column! Perfect for Laughing!

Advertisements are invading our lives through the airwaves and on the streets. Their ubiquity in society makes them nearly impossible to avoid, and I personally am repulsed by each one. In fact, the last time I was subjected to one for more than fifteen seconds, I became vomitously ill and repeatedly stabbed at my ears with a fountain pen.

Oh, wait. That's boy bands I'm thinking of. Sorry, wrong column.

Back to advertising. I'm sick of ads, commercials, sponsors, promotions, big sales, holiday sales, once-in-a-lifetime sales, sales pitches, sales people, sail boats and 10-10-220. Half of these advertisements don't even make much sense, at least not biblically speaking.

For example, I don't understand Cheetos bags. On every bag, it says in big letters, "Dangerously Cheesy!" The Cheetos company seems very proud of the fact that their product is dangerously cheesy. What does this mean? So cheesy it can cause a rash? So cheesy it can kill a man? How cheesy is it? They just come right out there and say that their product is dangerous. If they related dangerous to anything other than "cheesiness," it would be a whole different matter. I would not want Cheetos that were "dangerously unsanitary" or "dangerously cancerous."

Another example are Tostitos bags. They now makes bags of chips that say, "Bite Size! Perfect for dipping!" Were people really having that much trouble before bite size chips were available? Were they trying different ways to fit the entire Tostito in their mouth? Did they come back to the grocery store, "Listen, I bought these Tostitos and when I got home, I realized they just don't fit in my mouth. I can't figure out how to use them. They should come with instructions or something." There shouldn't even be "bite size" chips. There should just be regular chips that say on the side of the bag, "For Bite Size, kick the bag you IDIOT!" All you have to do is give it a couple good body slams, and you'll have plenty of "bite size" chips.

I also bought a blank tape recently with a package that boasted, "Perfect for recording!" That's good to hear because what else am I going to use a blank tape for? I don't really plan on playing Frisbee or slicing tomatoes with it. I think these advertising guys don't care what they put on the package. Soon you'll see books that say, "Perfect for reading!" and pants that say "Perfect for when you don't want to be naked!"

The most annoying product name is "I Can't Believe It's Not Butter." Since when can the name of a product be an opinion? You don't see "How Can Something That Tastes This Good Be A Laxative?" I, for one, *can* believe it's not butter, and I'm not going to stand for it any longer.

The most annoying commercials are those for Energizer batteries. Why is the Energizer bunny still going? So ten years ago, when he first started, we were sort of impressed. "Hey, look at that. The little bastard's still going. Good for him." But now we're just tired of it. We don't expect the bunny to stop. What do they want from us, a formal surrender? "We, the consumers, hereby proclaim that we understand the bunny keeps going and going . . . and going. We no longer doubt his marching abilities, and from now on we will buy only Energizer batteries." I think the best solution would be for the Energizer bunny to pull a Forest Gump—just suddenly stop and say, "Well, I'm kinda' tired. I think I'm gonna go home now."

Despite my ranting and raving, annoying advertisements will keep going and going and going. They will continue covering our television screens and invading our dreams. There will be a few smart souls who will gauge out their eyes with ice cream scoops, but the rest of us will have no choice but to continue to watch these diseases of the mind as they consume society and devour the livelihood of all mankind.

Wait, that's boy bands I'm thinking of again. My mistake. Well, advertisements are bad too.

Motor Oil Made of Four Leaf Clovers and Baby Unicorn Noses

There comes a point about every three months in a guy's life when he's sitting peacefully on a couch somewhere and an intrusive thought jumps into his head for better or worse. "I should probably get my oil changed." This thought has cursed men ever since the time of their acceptance into civilized society (1983 to be exact). It doesn't matter if the man knows nothing about cars, like how the cup holder functions, the words "oil change" will nonetheless begin blinking in his head like a strobe light. (This is not to say that women don't get their oil changed. I just imagine they take a much more logical approach to it.)

Men have had this problem for thousands of years. In fact, in early Egyptian times, wives and children would be left to fend for themselves for one week out of every three months while all the men in the society ran around aimlessly trying to figure out the meaning behind the thought, "I should probably get my oil changed."

On the other hand, modern-day men quickly try to distract ourselves when this thought attacks our minds. We turn on ESPN post haste and often succeed in forgetting about the thought for another month or two. However, at that point the thought launches a counteroffensive in the more convincing form of "I should *really* get my oil changed."

So those of use who don't know how to change it ourselves then head off to some sort of oil change facility which has "Jiffy," "Quickie" or "While You Wait" in its name. For the fifty percent of men that, like me, know very little about motor vehicles, this trip is quite intimidating. We have to hand our beloved vehicle over to a bunch of guys with names like Bull who then do lots of stuff to our car that we don't understand. This process feels similar to how it would feel if you brought your wife or girlfriend to a guy you'd never met before who somehow knew a hell of a lot more about her than you did. "Don't worry, man. I'll take her from here. I'll have her working right in no time."

The mechanics who work on your car always have at least two-thirds of each of their hands dyed black, which means either they work on car engines all day long or they never wash their hands (or, in most cases, both). These blackened hands actually serve as a form of intimidation to all the men who have never worked on a car engine and have never had blackened hands, excluding the one time we chewed a pen open when we were five. The intimidation factor stems from the fact that it was established long ago that men with dirty hands or clothes are to be considered far manlier than those with clean clothes and hands. For this reason, when we men come home from a neighborhood football game, we will proudly strut around the house in our muddy, sweat-stained clothes for hours, if not days, in an attempt to impress our wives or girlfriends. However, women apparently never received the memo that nastiness is manly, and most women will evacuate the premises long before we are done showing off.

When I arrived at Jiffy Lube for my latest oil change, I had to relinquish control of my car to several people I probably would not trust to water my bonsai tree for a weekend. Bull then came over and asked me complicated car questions such as what type of oil I wanted in my car. He listed five types of oils and made it sound like the only type that would give my car a fighting chance of making it back to my apartment in one piece was the fifty dollar deluxe brand made from four leaf clovers and baby unicorn noses. However, I had seen several "Dateline" reports in which unsuspecting idiots like myself were tricked into paying upwards of five dollars more than they should have. So I asked him about the less expensive brands.

Me: What about the ten dollar brand?
Bull: Well, it's not bad, but your car will blow up in a few days.
Me: Oh, well maybe I should get the twenty-five dollar brand.
Bull: That's a pretty good choice except it does tend to leak toxic fumes into the car but only if you drive it for longer than three minutes at a time.

It just so happened that I had a bottle of oil in the back of my car at the time. So I also asked if they could simply use the oil I already had. Their response to this was a long stretch of technical car terms including words like "capacitor" and "grommet." From what I gathered, he essentially said, "No, we don't like to do that because it could, under some circumstances, save you money. We'd prefer to pressure you into purchasing a brand new, very expensive bottle of oil." It sounded fair enough, so I agreed to whatever the man said and headed off to the waiting room feeling triumphant. I had asked a lot of pointless questions, and in my opinion that made me a well-informed consumer.

The small waiting room had a huge window allowing nervous customers to view the excessively expensive dismantling of their automobiles. The giant window made it feel like we were staring into a huge aquarium, except the fish were disemboweling my car – not something you normally ask of your fish.

The room also had a television tuned to some soap opera in order to remind all the customers that everybody in the world is filled with deceit and ulterior motives. This was not so comforting seeing as I had just entrusted my car to a man in a one-piece jump suit.

Eventually, a mechanic came into the waiting room holding what seemed to be either a piece of my car or some old food I had left in the back seat. The man told me it was my air filter and proceeded to pull open parts of it to show me that there was dirt inside, which meant it needed to be replaced. The truth is he could have been showing me someone else's air filter. Heck, he could have been showing me someone else's glove compartment, and I wouldn't have known the difference. In fact, he could have shown me a live koala bear and said that my air filter shouldn't have eyes, and I would have replied, "You're right. It does seem to have at least two eyes. Better replace that."

After twenty minutes, Bull called me out to give him a lot more of my money. He read a long list of car parts and what their status was in my car. If I remember correctly, he said, "Coolant – fine, oil – good, headlights – realigned, tires

– suck, windows – covered in bird poop, fan belt – we accidentally broke that, air filter – replaced with a koala bear, steering wheel – relocated to the trunk, passenger seat – soiled, engine – damned if we know. The total comes to . . . all the money you currently have in your wallet or one hundred dollars, whichever is greater."

I soon got out of there after being reunited with my car or one that looked similar. On the way home a light began flashing in the dashboard which read, "maint. reqd." I just assumed that was my car's way of saying "Thank you" in some unknown car language. I said, "You're welcome," and continued on my way.

What's inside A Battery? And Other Questions That Lead to Eye Trauma

I first realized I needed glasses half way through college. I began having difficulty seeing certain things like the writing on class room chalk boards. At first I insisted the fault was not my own. During several classes, I yelled to the professor, "Stop writing blurry!" On other occasions, I played it off like I could see things that I actually could not. "I saw that cow. I just ran over it because it gave me an ugly look."

I simply refused to believe my eyesight was declining. Eventually my roommate tried to force me past my denial.

Roommate: Lee, you need to get glasses.
Me: Who said that? Who's there? I do not need glasses! I'll take all five of you on!

I think my problem was that it's depressing to think my body is already fading while I'm still young. I was afraid that if I gave in to my weakening eyesight, before I knew it, I would be wearing pants short enough to show my ugly socks even when I was standing up, and I would adore Regis Philbin.

Anyway, I accepted the fact that I needed glasses and headed off to an eye doctor. Once there, I filled out a form concerning my vision, which unfortunately asked if I had a history of eye trauma. I say "unfortunately" because it's embarrassing to have to write, "I got acid in my eye when trying to smash open a battery." I might as well have written, "I'm a freaking moron lacking in common sense. Please pity my ignorant soul."

Since I previously obtained permission from my faithful readers to digress in this column (We had coffee this morning), I'll go ahead and explain how I got battery acid in my eye at the age of four. I wish I was making up the following story, but I'm not that lucky.

To put it simply, I wanted to understand the inner workings of a battery. Looking back on the experience, I can see how such an endeavor could be tempting. At that age we saw batteries go into every cool toy – remote control cars, talking Elmo, stun guns. But we had no idea what those batteries were doing in there or what they were made of. For all I knew, they had PEZ inside, and I felt I had an obligation to my fellow four-year-olds to crack this long-kept secret.

Truthfully, my thinking was probably more along the lines of, "Let's see . . . what in this room have I not yet smashed with a hammer? . . . The dog, but she'd probably make noise. You know what won't make noise? A battery! Not to mention there's a possibility of hidden PEZ."

So I wandered off to the shed because, even at that age, I knew that if a guy wants to build or dismantle something that his wife or parents would not approve of, it takes place in the shed. And I wasn't the only boy who knew that there were cool "off-limits" toys in the shed. In fact, when I walked into the shed that day, one of the walls was still partially brown from an incident involving my older brother and a can of spray paint.

So if things had gone as planned, I now would be informing you that I was the first person to uncover the icing-filled center of batteries, earning me the Nobel Prize for science at the age of four. But . . . things did not go as planned.

To my great surprise, slamming a battery with a hammer turned out to be a bad idea. When the acid sprayed in my eye, I ran to my dad, who was lying on the hammock relaxing and thinking about how life with children actually did have some peaceful moments. As I started to panic, my dad asked me how I got hurt. When he looked me in the eye (singular), I had no choice but to tell him the truth. I said (this is also true), "Dad . . . I ran into a bush." I have not been able to lie that well again, except for the time I told my roommate his bag of Cheetos was gone because it had been repossessed by the IRS while he was in the bathroom.

To make a long story a little longer, I went to the hospital but had very little damage to my eye. Then, my parents decided I was no longer allowed to smash things with a hammer unless my dad encouraged it, which turned out to be fairly often.

Getting back to a couple weeks ago, I was sitting in the eye doctor's office while she read over my chart, which included the phrase "smashed a battery with a hammer." I definitely didn't have to worry about trying to impress her.

The doctor then did some simple testing.

Doctor: Does it hurt when I poke you in the eye?
Me: Yes.
Doctor: How about if I use a pointy object?
Me: Yes.
Doctor: How about if I do it harder?
Me: Yes.

She soon decided my eyes weren't that bad. I guess God simply didn't punish me for the battery incident because he's either too busy or too lazy. I'm sure the paper work necessary to give someone extensive eye trauma is a bitch.

So I was off to buy my glasses. It immediately concerned me that the salesperson, who was supposed to help me choose eyewear, was sporting frames roughly the size and weight of an espresso machine. I know very little about glasses, but he apparently bought his from a yard sale at Drew Carey's house.

Because I had never worn glasses before, I didn't realize how expensive frames are. Why should there be frames that cost one hundred and fifty dollars? Should I really have to pay that much to look a little more like a nerd? Charging so much for frames is really just kicking a man when he's down. I had already been forced to confess my eyesight was declining, see a doctor and increase my overall nerd level, and now these people wanted to make me pay a lot for it? If you ask me, they should give you the frames for free along with a bag of cookies and a psychotherapy session.

I now have a pair of quasi-ugly glasses that I wear when I'm driving or when there's a partially naked woman on television. For anybody who was shocked by the last sentence, relax because I'm just kidding – I'm far too lazy to put on my glasses when I'm driving.

7 Statements Most Commonly Edited out of Infomercials

1. Should we tell them it causes a nasty rash?
2. Seven audience members got third-degree burns from the Chicken Roaster 2000, and it wasn't even turned on

3. And now Mandy will demonstrate the Health Rider while Bill and I try to avoid staring at her ass
4. Call 911. Susan vacu-sealed her head again!
5. Wait, why the hell am I cutting a shoe? Who cares if the knife can cut a damn shoe?
6. What kind of a sick person puts a cat in a bread maker?!
7. So you just sit in the Ab-Flexer like this, and it's simple to—Oh God! My stomach feels like it's on fire!! Oh dear, merciful Lord! Make the pain stop!!

Cuddly Bunny Rips Through Florida

I regret to bring to your attention yet another severe problem with this country, which everyone from our federal government down to Oprah has completely ignored and would seem to have us believe does not even exist: Rain. That's right, rain. Have you noticed this? There is water falling directly from the sky down onto us and those we care about, and nobody is doing a damn thing about it. In fact, right now I'd like to announce my candidacy for governor of Virginia with the platform, "No New Rain!"

No matter when you're reading this, much of the country is currently wetter than a four-year-old on a long road trip after finishing a Super Big Gulp. I have noticed that rain seems to be very frightening for many people. Everybody you see is ducking under trees, running inside buildings or carrying huge umbrellas. Evidently these people are waking up, voluntarily getting in the shower and allowing water to pour down onto them, and then running to their cars thinking, "Oh my God, I'm getting wet!" And I refuse to believe that it's because they don't want their clothes to get wet. What are these people wearing? A Rembrandt? Are they really getting home and going, "Oh no, I can't believe I got this shirt wet. Now, I have to soak it in water to get it clean again."

I don't like umbrellas either. As far as I can tell nobody has been able to come up with an umbrella that can last more than a month. Why is it that rain is making these things fall to pieces faster than American cars? I noticed recently that most people's umbrellas are half broken or at least have one pointy metal rod sticking out of the fabric. Maybe these exposed metal points act as an umbrella defense system to deter people from trying to "share" the umbrella. "Hey, can I get under this umbrel – Ow! My eye!" I also wonder what kind of deadly rain causes these umbrellas to just fall apart. I think if there is one object we might not want to get wet during a rain storm, it's our umbrellas because they just can't seem to handle it.

Weather is a serious problem, and some of the worst originates from hurricanes. But I often have trouble believing hurricanes can be destructive because of the stupid names we've been giving them. For example, a couple years ago we had hurricane Floyd. That's right, it's name was Floyd. How about Gert? Did you see that one? Sounds like you're choking on a small animal. Where are they getting these names? It's just an insult to know that your house was washed away by something named Floyd. Things named Floyd don't tear up coastlines; they cut hair in small southern towns.

The way I see it, meteorologists have two choices. The first is to name hurricanes after horrible things. For example, "Hurricane McVeigh," or "Hurricane *That 70's Show*." This way, people would be comfortable hating hurricanes. The other choice is to name the hurricanes after really cute things, so that at least the news casts would be entertaining. The news reports would then be like, "We have confirmed reports that Cuddly Bunny ripped through Florida injuring at least forty people, and it's not over yet because Baby's Bottom is right behind it. No pun intended, folks."

You also have to question the sanity of weather correspondents. When these guys are reporting from a hurricane, every television viewer is not listening to what they're saying but instead thinking, "What the hell are those guys doing there?"

News Anchor: Let's check in with Bill who's actually on the coast of South Carolina right now.
Correspondent: Janet, the winds are definitely picking up! Trees are down all over the place! Every sane human being was evacuated from this area hours ago. My eyes feel like they're being pressed back into my head! The rain drops are actually making me bleed! I'm sorry I have to yell in order to hear myself, but my ears were blown off just minutes ago! Oh, this just in – a piece of sharp, rusty metal, possibly ripped off a building nearby, just lodged itself deep into my thigh! But this is all worth it because I'm able to tell the nation th—
News Anchor: Looks like we lost the audio feed. Wow, Bill sure is getting hit hard by that weather. Speaking of hits, let's go to Ed with some baseball scores!

Read my lips: No More Rain! *Lee Camp for governor.*

11

Fiction

Personal Thoughts

(Inside Dan's head – these are his thoughts. It is completely dark except for a spotlight on Dan.)

Dan

Hello, is this thing on? Wait, I'm just thinking. I guess there's no need for a microphone. Anyway—

Ed

Okay, it's on. Say "testing" or something so I can see how it sounds.

Dan

What the hell? These are my thoughts to myself. I don't need a microphone.

Ed (to himself)

Jesus, why do I always get the freaks?

Ed (to Dan)

Listen man, if you don't test the mike, it's gonna sound like crap during the show, and the audience will blame me. I'm getting paid five twenty-five an hour for this crap, and I don't need pissed off people to deal with. So just talk into the microphone.

Dan
Show? I have to do a show? I haven't prepared anything. Wait, who are you and what the hell are you doing in my head?

Ed
I was hired by Earl. Now, would you just talk into the microphone? We've only got five minutes before the people get here, so can we speed it up?

Dan (confused, into the microphone)
Testing. Testing, one, two.

Ed (while adjusting the sound)
Good job, keep talking. Do some of your speech. I've always wondered about comprehending the universe in terms of home improvement. Isn't that what you're going to speak about?

Dan
What? I have to speak? I haven't prepared anythi—

Ed
Remember that whole discussion we had about talking into the microphone? Let's apply the results here.

Dan (more confused, into the microphone)
But I don't have anything prepared. I don't know anything about the universe or home improvement. . . . Well, I have

always said that the universe is like a giant deck except there's nowhere to hang a hammock.

Ed
Alright, that'll do it. Thanks, Dan. Good luck on the speech. I definitely respect what you do. I can't imagine speaking in front of hundreds of people.

Dan
Hundreds?! It's my own damn mind! I didn't invite hundreds of people. I just wanted to sit down and think about that hot chick at work, not give a speech. . . . Okay, I just need to relax. I can get out of this. Hey Ed, where's that Earl guy that you said hired you?

Ed
Haven't you already answered your own question?

Dan
What the hell are you talking about? No, I didn't—wait, maybe I have. Maybe I'm having a spiritual awakening. That's what this is. You're here to guide me to the answers which have always been laying dormant in my soul. Guide me, Ed. I'm ready now. I'm ready for the true answers!

Ed
I'm just messin' with ya. Earl's in the crapper, I think.

Dan
Oh . . . Alright, I get it. I just need to think myself out of this. None of this is really here. This stage isn't really here. This microphone isn't really here. This guy Ed isn't really here. It's all in my imagination. It's all—

Ed

Could you hand me that wire that isn't really by your left foot?

Dan (handing Ed the wire)

Here ya go. This wire isn't really here. That bar isn't really over in that corner. None of this is here. I'm sitting in my chair, at home, thinking about Linda from work. Today she said hi to me. That happened in real life. This is not real.

(*Earl Enters*)

Earl (to Ed)

What the hell is he doing?

Ed

I think it's some kind of meditation or else it might be the Tequila.

Dan

I'm not meditating! These are my thoughts! What are you doing here?!

Earl

You must be Dan. Good ta have ya here. My friend Surly told me you were a kooky one. But hey, as long as you give a good speech, I don't care if ya get ready for the show by molesting waterfowl. You do whatever you gotta do.

Dan

There is no show! I just wanted to drink a beer by myself!

Earl (yelling across the room)

Billy, get this man a cold one! Get him that new import that just came in!

Billy (from across the room)
Anything you say, boss.

Dan
No, I mean I want to be drinking a beer at my house.

Earl
And I want my wife to tell me I have to have an affair with a Playboy bunny in order to save our marriage, but it ain't in the cards, kid. Anyway, you're up in twenty. Good luck.

Dan
Wait, Earl. What the hell is this place? I'm not supposed to be here.

Earl
We already went through this over the phone. But you seem a little out of it tonight, so I'll run it by ya again. This is my club. We've been doin' entertainment acts every Friday night for the past five years. You know, comedians, ventriloquists, clowns, that kind of thing. The crowd has enjoyed it, but a lot of the customers said they wanted something a little more sophisticated.

Dan
Really?

Earl
The clowns just weren't doing it for them intellectually. I knew it was time for a change about three weeks ago when there was this juggling number up on stage, and the audience members started yelling out questions. You know, "Would you consider yourself more liberal or conservative?," "Do you feel Marx was right in his statement that Realist art was the only form of art that supported the bourgeois when,

in fact, Realism was at least partially subjective?" That kind of thing. When the two jugglers said Marx was not justified, the crowd went into an uproar, throwing chairs, paying less than fifteen percent tip, etc. It was a mess. So, you're the first of the speakers I've hired to give the people what they want. We'll see how it goes. I'm expecting at least two hundred people tonight. Well, I gotta go make some phone calls. Knock 'em dead, kid.

(*Earl leaves*)

Dan

Wait, Earl—

Linda

Hey Dan.

Dan

Linda? Oh, thank God. That means things are getting back to normal. I meant to be thinking about you all along.

Linda

Listen Dan, I've read your book, and I was wondering . . . if the universe is simply a giant tool belt, as you insist, why are the needle nose pliers always falling out?

Dan

What? I have a book? I have no idea why the pliers fall out. What are you talking about?

Linda

Jeeze, Dan. If you don't know the answer to a simple question like that, the audience is gonna' get pretty angry. I'll see ya after the show. Good luck.

(*Linda exits.*)

Dan

Wait! This is insane. Okay, just calm down. None of this is real. I'm at my house by myself. There's no reason to be worried because none of this exists. I'm not here. I'm not—

Alice

Mr. Fitzpatrick, my name's Alice. I'm a big fan. I just find your writing soooo incredible. Listen, I have an apartment a couple blocks from here if you want to come get some coffee after—

Dan

Let me grab my coat.

(As Dan and Alice are walking out together . . .)

Dan

So what do you think of my book? Pretty intelligent stuff, huh?

THE END

~~Alone with My Thoughts~~ ~~Immortal Words~~ Diary

7/18 I am beginning to get delirious. I see water all around me, but when I reach for it, an angry person tells me to get a glass of my own. I hardly know where I am anymore. I must get fresh water soon or all is lost. My tongue feels dry and blistered. I've never felt such oppressive heat in all my life. Having eaten my entire rations of bread and crackers, I have no food left either. Soon my stomach will begin to ravage my insides. I fear death is not far off. **Note for anybody who may read this diary following my imminent demise:** Never eat at Angelo's Pasta Palace. The service here is horrible. How hard could it be to bring a glass of water?

7/18 (update) Well, they finally brought the water, but they forgot the lemon that I asked for. I refuse to drink water without a lemon wedge. **Further note for anybody who may read this diary following my imminent demise:** If you insist on eating here, bring your own lemon and a book to help pass the time. I brought some medicine labels that I wanted to catch up on, but I have long since gotten bored by them.

8/12 I have met the woman of my dreams. It took seventy-five years, but it has finally happened. I paid for her today on my way home from the store. I truly feel love. She went to the bathroom on the carpet this afternoon but made up for it by eating that mouse that had been living in my pantry. I'm still trying to find out if it is legal in this state for a man to marry a Scottish terrier.

8/15 I played chess today with my good buddy Gene Hatterford. Just as I was about to win, he insisted that a straight flush always beats two of a kind. I tried to explain that we were not playing poker, and he said that was beside the point. We argued for the better part of an hour before Gene became frustrated and dunked all the rooks in chocolate milk before feeding them to his dog. For a moment I was distraught with the realization that Gene had lost his mind. However, following our dispute, he went to sleep in the laundry shoot, and I knew it was the same old Gene.

8/23
-cream
-bologna
-~~relish~~
-moon pies
-those little things to fix with the yogurt
-8 pounds of knockwurst
-two bags of rabbit food (the kind she likes)
-a rabbit

Ignore the above list. **Note to self**: Keep diary and grocery list more clearly marked.

9/5 Today I was a little frightened when I thought I heard a voice coming from my closet. This surprised me because the closet hasn't spoken to me since an argument we had twenty years ago. I thought for a moment that there was someone hiding in the closet, perhaps a burglar or a Jehovah's Witness. As I slowly opened the closet door, expecting to find that the voice was coming from some unusual person inside, I was relieved to see that it was only an old sweater. It was muttering to itself about the humidity.

9/7 I awoke today to find that I was somehow receiving the porn channel on my television for free. What a country! This type of happiness can only be found in America, and it is exactly the reason my great grandfather moved here from Poland in the 1800's. Although there was no volume, I could do nothing for two hours other than watch a sporty young couple go at it on my television. My luck came to an end when the couple suddenly looked straight at the camera man, became infuriated, and began flicking him off. It was then that I realized I had merely been watching the next door neighbors through their window. This was slightly shocking but did not change the fact that the show had been free.

9/21 This morning I could not find my car keys. I could have sworn I left them in the cheddar cheese like always but they weren't there. I continued to look all over the house for them until I found an old lava lamp which I was captivated by until I got ready to go to bed just now.

9/22 I still could not find the keys to my car but luckily found the keys to my motorcycle, which I don't ride much anymore. I decided that it would have to do, and I attempted to drive it to the market. Three hours later with little success, I remembered that I don't own a motorcycle, and I had been riding my stationary bike.

9/24 I gave up on finding the car keys and instead pushed the car into a nearby lake. It was a piece of crap anyway. (The last time I tried to kill myself with the exhaust fumes I couldn't get it started.) I plan to use a tricycle I stole from a four-year-old as my only form of transportation. The other big news today is that I have finally begun work on project Alpha Omega. Once completed, it will surely change the lives of every human being. Unfortunately all I have done so far is think of the name and draw up a few blue prints. . . . Well, since this is my personal diary I should confess that I thought of the name first and then decided there should be a project to go along with it. In fact, there are no blue prints yet. I'm not yet sure what the project is going to consist of. . . . I'm not even sure I thought up the name. It may be something I saw in a science fiction movie.

9/25 Further work on project Alpha Omega has been cancelled. On a brighter note I spent less than an hour on the toilet today, breaking my old personal best set in 1973.

11/27 Sorry I haven't written for about two months. I was busy going through the mail and such.

11/28 Linda's her name. She's this incredible woman I met at bingo last night. She may be a year younger than me, but I hear younger women are energetic in bed. Well, I'm getting ahead of myself. I should talk to her first. I need to take this relationship slowly so that it'll work out better than my last one. Five years ago I was madly in love, and everything was going right. But then we started drifting apart. I don't know why. It was surprisingly hard to have a truly intimate relationship since I wasn't allowed within two hundred yards of her due to laws that I won't get into right now. Anyway, I know it will work out this time. Linda is without a doubt the most wonderful woman I've ever met. Oh, Linda . . . What a beautiful name. Or maybe her name was Emily. What a beautiful name.

12/5 Things didn't work out with Emily. Maybe I'm gay . . . **Note to self**: call all three ex-wives and eight children to let them know. Better yet, send a Hallmark card.

12/6 Don't think I'm gay anymore. I watched an old James Bond movie, and Sean Connery didn't do it for me. **Note to self**: take back all those scented candles and posters of babies and send out "Not Gay Anymore" Hallmark cards.

12/7 Need to start Christmas shopping. If I don't buy presents soon, all the good stuff will be gone. And then all my friends will be sitting around going, "What's up with that jerk, he didn't buy me anything!" And I'll try to tell them that everything was already gone. But it'll be too late because they'll already hate me, and they'll start treating me bad. Those bastards! They're gonna hate me? After all I've done for them?!! I can't believe this! I'll show them – I'm gonna go take back their gifts right now!

12/18 My heel started aching today. It was incredibly painful and persisted for a long period of time. I eventually went to see a doctor. After what seemed like several hours of testing, he told me to stop wearing women's shoes. Sure enough that cleared it right up. However, now I don't have anything to wear that will go with my blue blouse.

12/22 Christmas is approaching. I can't wait to see my two kids. I'm driving to one of their houses on Christmas eve. Should be fun. My daughter and her family only have a small house, so I usually sleep in the front yard when I visit, but it's still great to see them. Anyway, I'm really looking forward to it. I bought her the greatest gift. It's a moisturizer dispenser shaped like a penguin . . . wait, that's for me. Anyway, I got her something too. Okay, I gotta' go wrap presents.

12/28 Damn it! I overslept and missed Christmas and the three days directly following it. I think what happened is that instead of putting my alarm clock next to my bed and setting it for 8:00 am, I accidentally put the toaster oven next to my bed and set it for 800 degrees.

1/5 I just watched a great college bowl game! It was a hell of a thing. I don't remember who played but one of the mascots was a bird. A bird in a football player's uniform! Can you believe it? Birds don't wear football uniforms! (Well, there was that one five months ago. But we had a discussion, and he agreed never to do it again.)

1/13 Had a horrible dream that I got married to a praying mantis, and it eventually ate our children. This upset me greatly seeing as I had spent days building the children's crib from scratch, and then we had no use for it. However, we worked out our marital problems, and overall she was surprisingly more cordial than my first wife as well as a better cook. I awoke relieved that my children had not been eaten but somewhat disappointed I no longer had the companionship of the praying mantis.

1/15 I was robbed blind today. I have to give the thieves credit though. It was an ingenuous scam. A couple of little girls came to my door asking if I wanted to buy girl scout cookies. I said sure, and I went to find my wallet. When I got back to the door, it turned out that the little girls weren't girl scouts at all—they were thirty-five-year-old men with baseball bats. Now that I think about it, I should've figured it out since they were much taller than me, and one had a beard. But then again, they were wearing the little uniforms, and how embarrassing would it have been if I had accused them of being thirty-five-year-old men, and they had actually been girl scouts. I would have crushed the poor girls, and the tall girls with facial hair get made fun of a lot in school anyway. So, long story short, the men asked if they could take all my stuff, and I agreed because they didn't seem like the type who take rejection very well. On the plus side, they did leave me a box of mint cookies. I find the whole incident less painful if I just pretend that I paid a great deal for the cookies.

2/14 Today I find myself overcome with guilt. I'm afraid I haven't been completely honest with you, my Dear Diary. The first entry in you did indeed occur on July 18, 2000. However, I wrote all of the rest of the entries yesterday in order to make up for the several months I missed. That's not to say that the vast majority of what I described in those entries did not take place. It simply means it all took place yesterday. I regret to inform you also, Dear Diary, that this will be my last entry. Besides the fact that I am jaded by the process of keeping a diary because of all the treachery that is involved, I am also almost out of ink in this pen. And to be quite honest, I don't see myself getting up the energy to buy another pen for quite some time. Goodbye. You will be well missed.

BVG